Miss Frost
Cracks ᵃ Caper

A Nocturne Falls Mystery
Jayne Frost, book four

KRISTEN PAINTER

MISS FROST CRACKS A CAPER
A Nocturne Falls Mystery
Jayne Frost, Book Four

Copyright © 2017 Kristen Painter

This book is a work of fiction. The characters, events, and places portrayed in this book are products of the author's imagination and are either fictitious or are used fictitiously. Any similarity to real person, living or dead, is purely coincidental and not intended by the author.

ISBN: 978-1-941695-32-6

Published in the United States of America.

Welcome to Nocturne Falls — the town that celebrates Halloween 365 days a year.

Jayne Frost is a lot of things. Winter elf, Jack Frost's daughter, Santa Claus's niece, heir to the Winter Throne and now...private investigator. Sort of.

When Lark Bramble, an old frenemy, shows up in Nocturne Falls, Jayne finds herself reliving the painful past and trying to make responsible decisions that won't mess up her future. But being an adult proves harder than she thought.

Finally at peace with where things stand between her and Lark, Jayne thinks everything's cool until a chilling event at the Black and Orange Ball shatters that peace and puts Jayne at odds with the powers that be. She knows she's on thin ice, but she's determined to crack the caper.

Can Jayne find a way to right the wrongs she might have caused or will she forever bear the guilt of allowing herself to be snowed again?

The bells over the shop door jangled again, but the two men in front of me, Greyson Garrett and Cooper Sullivan, blocked my view.

I gave them both a stern look. "I have customers to take care of, so you two are going to have to—"

"Well, well. Am I interrupting a party?"

At the sound of that voice, Cooper and I stared at each other like we'd just heard a ghost. I put my hands on the guys' shoulders and pushed them apart like curtains.

I stared at the woman who'd just walked in. After the day I'd had, I wasn't sure I could believe my eyes. Or that I wanted to. My mouth went dry, but I managed one word: "Lark?"

She laughed, throwing her head back in that way she'd always had. "Surprised to see me?"

I swallowed and found my voice, despite the

storm of emotions rolling through me. "More than I can say."

Lark.

Was here.

In Nocturne Falls.

In my shop.

Her once long silver hair had been cut into a hip asymmetrical bob, and the underlying layer was now a deep glacial blue, but the woman in front of me was definitely Lark. I just stared, hoping that any second I'd wake up. I pinched my leg. *Ow.* Nope, not waking up. This was real.

Lark was standing in front of me.

Yeti poop. Big steaming piles of it.

She smiled at me like it hadn't been nearly ten years since we'd seen each other. Like she hadn't been the reason that Cooper and I broke up. "Long time no see, Jaynie."

Like she hadn't tried to seduce him immediately afterward.

She blinked a few times when I didn't answer and tried again. "So how have you been?"

I reminded myself she didn't know Cooper and I had talked that all out since I'd arrived in Nocturne Falls. But I still had no words. I literally couldn't think of a single thing to say.

Apparently, neither could Cooper, because he was just as quiet as I was. Greyson, thankfully, wasn't having that problem.

He stuck his hand out. "Greyson Garrett. And you are?"

"Lark Bramble. But DJ Ice Queen is my professional name. That's why I'm here, actually. The DJ part."

"Oh?" Greyson kept going, saving me the trouble of becoming conversational.

"Looks like I'm going to be doing a big party here in October. The Black and Orange Ball? I was told it's a major event every year."

A couple came in, and Juniper went to help them. I appreciated that because I knew she'd rather hang out and listen in on this awkward situation. Of course, she knew I'd fill her in later, and she was nothing if not a great employee.

Greyson nodded. "The Black and Orange Ball is *the* event in Nocturne Falls."

"How cool. Have you been?"

"Yes, several times."

The small talk was kind of getting to me. This whole acting like nothing had ever happened between us might have been okay for the person I used to be, but my time and responsibilities in Nocturne Falls had changed me. I finally broke my silence. "Why are you here, Lark?"

She looked at me, uncertainty taking the brightness off her smile. "I told you, I'm potentially going to be DJing at this gala in October of next year. I'm here now to work out all the details with the woman who puts it on. Elenora Ellingham. Do you know her?"

Greyson answered for me. "Jayne knows everyone in town. And they know her."

Not entirely true, but I got what he was doing and was definitely giving him points for it.

"Well, this Elenora is really something," Lark went on. "I'm going to tour the space tomorrow and tell her what kind of show I can provide. Get the contracts started. That sort of thing."

I wasn't buying it. Elenora Ellingham didn't seem like the type to hire a DJ for her famous Black and Orange Ball. It was an elegant affair, not a rave. "Really? A DJ at her renowned Halloween gala? That doesn't seem like Elenora at all."

Lark's smile finally disappeared altogether. "I don't just play songs, you know. I bring a whole show. I'm very well-known for my performances." She sighed and looked away for a moment, like facing me had suddenly become unbearable. "Look, I was hoping we could…talk. You and me. And Cooper, too, but to start with, just you and me. There's a lot we need—I need to say."

That was an understatement. But I wasn't about to open my arms and forgive her just yet, either. "Convenient timing, what with you here for a job and all."

She shrugged. "It is. But getting called about this job made me research the town. That's when I found out you—and Cooper—were in Nocturne Falls. It was the wake-up call I needed. It shook me out of the status quo and got me thinking. We were such good friends once upon a time."

"We *were*."

She gave Cooper a quick glance and a tentative smile that he did not return. "Could we please go somewhere and talk? I'm guessing you and Cooper have already done that, based on finding you together."

I stared at her. My emotions were a mess. We *had* been such good friends. At least, I thought that's what we'd been until she'd ruined my life. Sure, my life was great now, but when I was in college, she'd turned my life into a black hole. I hadn't known she was the one responsible then, but I did now.

I'd been wrecked by the breakup with Cooper. Heartbroken, miserable, and sure I'd never be loved again. You know, typical youthful angst. I'd gone home for Christmas, a time that was usually an endless celebration for me, and moped. Hard.

I ate ten pounds of my aunt's eggnog fudge that week. I wasn't proud of that, but I thought it proved just how despondent I was, seeing as how that was easily eight pounds more than normal. Okay, maybe seven, but still.

Cooper had been my future up until that moment.

Being reunited with him in Nocturne Falls had been great, outside of the fact that after we figured out Lark's part in our split, he also told me Lark had tried to seduce him.

So yeah, I had a lot of reasons not to talk to her. But I was an adult. And maybe a little bit curious about what she had to say. "I can't leave Juniper in the shop by herself. But I'll meet you for dinner at Howler's at seven. You know where that is?"

Her uncertain expression shifted back to the happy smile she'd had earlier. "Yes. Great. I'll be there. Thank you."

She started forward like she might hug me. I backed up. "Don't thank me yet."

She laughed it off. "Okay, see you then."

I nodded. She gave Cooper a little wave as she left. He didn't return the gesture.

A long moment of silence passed before anyone spoke again.

Cooper took a deep breath. "What the hell do you think she wants?"

"Beats me. I guess I'll find out at dinner."

He shook his head. "I can't believe she showed up here. She's got some nerve."

Greyson crossed his arms. "Who is this woman?"

Cooper ran a hand through his hair. "She was Jayne's best friend in college. She's also the reason we broke up."

I put my hands on my hips. "Don't forget how she tried to make you her boyfriend."

Cooper's eyes lit with dark fire. "How could I? It's not every day your ex-girlfriend's BFF shows up naked in your dorm room bed."

Greyson snorted. "I knew I should have gone to college."

I tipped my head at him. "Hey, funny boy, maybe you could find out if Elenora is really interested in her, or if Lark made that DJ story up."

He pressed his lips together in what looked like an attempt to stop smiling. "I can absolutely do that. I'll text you." He leaned in and kissed my cheek. "See you later."

As he left, Cooper leaned against the sales counter. "You want me to go to dinner with you?"

"Yes, but no. She's expecting to talk to me alone. I can handle it."

"Okay. You can always call me after."

"I will. Although I wouldn't be surprised if Lark contacts you. We already know she has your number."

"Yeah. Unfortunately. Can I do anything for you?"

I wasn't sure if that comment was because I'd given Greyson a task, but I had my suspicions. "No, thank you. I'm good. Exhausted, but good." It had been an extremely long day already. And the night probably wouldn't be much better.

7

He rubbed the back of his neck. "Well, if you don't mind, I'm going to find myself a seat at Howler's bar around seven. Just to keep an eye on things."

I smiled and shook my head. "I don't mind at all."

"Good." He winked, then leaned in and kissed me on the opposite cheek that Greyson had. "See you then."

"See you." I watched him go, greeting the customers who came in as he held the door.

Juniper sidled up to me. "So. What was that all about?"

"I have no idea. But that was Lark."

"The one who broke you and Coop up?"

"The very one."

"Huh. I thought she'd be some bombshell. I mean, she's pretty and all, but..." Juniper shrugged. "She's no you."

I smiled. "Thanks, but Lark did okay in college. She just couldn't get the one guy she really wanted."

"Cooper."

"Yep." I yawned. "I wish Vale and Crystal were here already." The two temps my dad had promised to send to help with the holiday rush would make my life bearable during the Christmas season.

"You could always hire another part-time

employee for the rest of the year." Juniper went behind the counter. "I could train them. Or Buttercup could."

"Maybe I'll run that past my dad tomorrow."

"That's not going to do you any good right now." Juniper frowned. "You're beat. Call Rowley in."

Rowley was our newest, and oldest, employee. He worked *only* part time. "It's his day off."

"Oh, he'd come in."

"I know he would, but I'm pretty sure he and his wife were going out of town today."

"So ask Buttercup to come in early. You know she would."

I did know that. But that wasn't fair to Buttercup. And seeing Lark reminded me of just how unfair life already was. "No, I'm good. I just need a Dr Pepper."

Juniper shook her head. "You're going to fall asleep at dinner. You shouldn't have sent Kip home."

"Not with Lark sitting across from me. And Kip was worse off than I am." He'd been doing double duty for me while I was dealing with the kidnapping of the shop's most recent visitor, Tempus Sanders aka the Sandman.

Juniper laughed. "I guess that's true. Lark will keep you awake. Go get your Pepper while it's slow, then."

"Yes, boss."

She stuck her tongue out at me as I headed back to the employee break room and its well-stocked fridge.

Lark Bramble was in town. And we were having dinner.

The weird just never quit in Nocturne Falls.

I made it through the shift without crashing, but the shower I took when I got back to my apartment really gave me my second wind. Also, I've never been so grateful that my father and uncle had the forethought to buy the entire building the shop and warehouse were located in and convert the upper floors into employee housing.

Not having to do more than ride the elevator up to get home was awesome.

Birdie called as I was standing in my closet figuring out what to wear to dinner with Lark. I grabbed my cell phone off my dresser. "Hey, Birdie, what's up?"

"I heard your little friend is in town."

She knew all about Lark. "Yes. And it's weird. But we're going to dinner to talk."

"Leopards don't change their spots."

"I agree, but I'm keeping an open mind."

Birdie hmphed. "Well, keep your guard up."

"I will, promise. Talk to you soon."

"Wait! That's not what I called about. We think there's a shoplifter in town. Willa just called in that she had a handful of Nocturne Falls pumpkin charms go missing from one of the cases in her store. Better tell your folks to pay extra attention to who's in the shop for a while."

I doubted anyone interested in jewelry was going to hit up the toy store next, but you never knew. "Thanks for the tip. I'll tell them to keep their eyes open."

"Okay. Have a good night. Talk to you soon. I'm going to want to hear all the dirt."

I laughed. "I have no doubt." I hung up, then sent a text to Buttercup about the shoplifter so she could be on the lookout during the evening shift.

With that handled, I changed into a sleek little yellow dress with a royal blue sweater coat. Both went well with my dark blue hair, but it was a bold statement. And not the kind of outfit college me would have worn.

And yes, I knew I was sending Lark a signal. That was the point. I needed her to understand she wasn't dealing with college Jayne. This was the new me. The me who was dating two guys and running her own shop and living her best life in a town that rocked.

I flicked on another layer of mascara.

Spider came and sat in the bathroom doorway and squinted up at me. "Mama bright."

I laughed. "I didn't think cats could see much in the way of color."

He gave me a harder look. "Mama bright." Then he sauntered into the bedroom.

Did I mention I have a talking cat? Well, I do. He didn't always talk, but I was accidentally granted a wish, and anyway, it stuck.

I shook my head and smiled. I loved that little black beasty. He'd probably be curled up on the bed and fast asleep in a few minutes. I'd fed him as soon as I'd gotten home, and he'd promptly cleaned out the bowl.

That was my boy. My Spider. The one and only talking cat. At least the only one I knew about.

I ran a brush through my hair and decided I was ready. I just needed some earrings and my purse. Both were on my dresser in the bedroom. As suspected, Spider had already settled on the bed.

He rolled over as I approached, a clear indicator that he expected a belly rub. Which, naturally, he got.

"Be a good boy while Mama's gone. I won't be too long." And I wouldn't be. No matter how much talking Lark wanted to do, I was going to be home by eight thirty. And in bed by nine.

"Spider loves bright Mama."

I giggled, a little punch drunk from lack of sleep. "Silly thing. I love you too." I kissed his head, then grabbed my earrings and purse and headed out.

With my purse tucked under my arm, I put the diamond hoops on in the elevator. Howler's was a short walk from the building that housed Santa's Workshop, the warehouse, and the employee apartments, which was part of why I ate there so much. Also, the food was fantastic.

The evening was brisk, just the kind of weather a winter elf loved. My sweater coat was plenty to keep me comfortable, and the cool air helped me wake up. My phone vibrated right before I stepped into the restaurant.

I checked the screen. It was a text from Greyson.

The DJ gig is legit.

Thanks, I texted back. That was interesting. And a real departure for Elenora's usual style, but then, Elenora was anything but boring.

Howler's was busy, as usual, but Bridget, the owner and a lovely werewolf, gave me a wave from behind the bar. I waved back. She nodded like she knew what was up. Cooper was already there, so I assumed he'd filled her in.

She pointed toward the right side of the restaurant. One of the booths had a RESERVED tent card on it. I pointed at it, then back at myself.

Bridget gave me the thumbs-up.

Thank you, I mouthed. That was very kind of her.

The hostess came back from seating another party. "Welcome to Howler's. Table for one?"

"Booth for two, actually. Bridget reserved one for me."

The girl smiled brightly. "You must be Miss Frost. Right this way."

"Thank you." I was a few minutes early, which I'd intended. I wanted to sit where I could see the door, not with my back to it. I slid into the booth and took the menu the hostess offered.

"Your server will be right with you."

As she walked away, my attention shifted to the door. Then my watch. I'd thought Lark would be early too. It was her idea to talk, after all. But she wasn't as familiar with this town as I was, so maybe she'd misjudged how long it would take her to get to Howler's.

I wondered where she was staying.

I wondered what her excuse was going to be.

The server came by, another bright-eyed college-age girl. She put two waters down. "Hi there, I'm Mia, I'll be your server this evening. Can I get you something to drink while you wait for the rest of your party?"

I was about to ask for a Dr Pepper when Lark came in. "She's here. Give us a minute or two."

"No problem." Mia left.

Lark was in silver Doc Martens, ripped boyfriend jeans, a faded band T-shirt, and a sleek black leather jacket. She looked terminally cool, and I felt overdressed and under-hip.

The hostess gestured at the table. "There you go. Enjoy your dinner."

"Thanks." Lark scooted onto the seat across from me. "Hi, you look so nice. I look like a bum."

"Thanks." I decided not to comment further on what we were wearing, opting instead to keep my voice and my expression neutral. "And hi." But inside, I was all wound up again. Clearly, I wasn't as over her betrayal as I'd thought. Or maybe it was just that being this close to her, facing her, was stirring up all my feelings again. Either way, my appetite was quickly disappearing.

Not something that often happened to me.

Lark picked up her menu. "So, what's good here?"

"Everything." I was getting the bacon cheeseburger. With fries. And topping it off with peach cobbler, although I'd probably be taking that with me so I could eat it in my jammies on the couch. Or possibly in bed. Don't judge. After the day I'd had, I needed comfort food.

"I wasn't sure what to expect." Lark glanced over the menu at me. "This place kind of looks like a biker bar from the outside. And a little on the inside too."

I put my menu down as Mia came back to take our order. "Hello, ladies. What can I get you to drink?"

Lark didn't seem quite ready, but I wasn't in a patient mood. "I'll have a Dr Pepper. And I'm ready to order, if that's okay?"

"Sure thing."

"Great. I'll have the bacon cheeseburger, medium, with everything and fries."

Mia scribbled on her notepad. "Perfect, got it. And for you, ma'am?"

Lark made a face. Maybe she didn't like being called ma'am. "I'll just have the veggie burger, no cheese, and sweet potato fries. And water is fine for me."

We handed our menus over to Mia. "I'll get those right in for you."

She bopped off, leaving Lark and me alone.

I laced my fingers together and set them on the table, but didn't say anything. It was a technique I'd learned from my dad. But being stared down by Jack Frost was probably enough to make most people talk. I hadn't quite mastered that level of intimidation.

Still, it seemed to work.

Lark smiled nervously. "So, you and Cooper are back together?"

"Not exactly. We date. I also date Greyson."

She frowned.

"The vampire you spoke with in my shop."

Her brows went up. Point for Jayne. "You're dating both of them? And they don't mind?"

I shrugged like I was an international woman of mystery. "They're cool with it. But we didn't come here to discuss my current dating life."

"No, I suppose not." Lark chewed on her bottom lip. "I don't even know where to start."

"How about the beginning?" To help her along, I added, "Why did you tell Cooper and me those lies to break us up? That was a pretty low thing to do considering I thought you were my best friend."

She was staring at the table. "I know. It was awful. Low is right. And there's no excuse for it. I was just young and dumb and thinking only about myself."

"Why would you do it, though? Did you really want Cooper that badly?"

She hesitated, then looked up at me. "Since I'm being honest here, I did it because I was horribly jealous of you."

I jerked back out of surprise. "We were best friends. We had almost identical class schedules. We ate together. We shared clothes, books, music, everything." Everything but Cooper. "Why would you be jealous of me?"

She exhaled like that was a dumb question. "Jayne, you were—and still are—the Winter Princess. You're North Pole royalty. Your father is Jack Frost and your uncle is Santa Claus. You have one of the most outstanding royal bloodlines in the history of royal bloodlines. I promise I'm not the only one who's ever been jealous of you."

"Well, your family has rank. And money." Her parents were toy scouts. They traveled the globe looking for new toy ideas to buy. It was a very prestigious job. "It's not like you were hurting in that department."

Mia came back with my Dr Pepper and Lark's water. Lark waited until she was gone to answer.

"It wasn't about money. It was about all the other stuff. The way people treated you. The way they looked at you. As if you were above everyone else. As if you could do no wrong. You were like a celebrity to them. Nobody cared who I was next to you."

I wanted to say she was making all of that up, but she wasn't. When word had gotten around in the supernatural population on campus about who I was, I'd definitely been treated differently. Not always for the better, mind you. But it wasn't like I'd had anything to do with my royal bloodlines. "You realize Winter Princess is a title I was born with. Not like I could change it if I wanted to."

Lark nodded. "I get it. Now. But then? I just wanted to be you. To live your life."

A sudden, painful realization hit me. "Is that why you became my friend?"

"No, I swear it wasn't. What drew us together was real."

We'd known each other growing up, but we hadn't been best friends as kids. The North Pole was a big place with the sensibilities of a small town. Wasn't until we found out we were headed to the same college that we bonded. Two winter elves against the world, as it were. "So you're telling me that jealousy drove you to betray me and destroy what you claim was a genuine friendship. Am I supposed to forgive that? Is that the purpose of this? So we can be friends again?"

She chewed on her lower lip, and so help me, I thought she might cry. That punched me in the heart a little. "I don't know what I expect to happen here. I just felt like it was time we talked."

I took a breath and tried to find some chill, but I wasn't done. I had questions that still needed answers. "So if Cooper and I hadn't figured out what you'd done, which you've obviously realized we have, your plan was to come here and confess everything?"

"Yes. That's exactly what I was going to do."

Easy to say. But would she really have? Who knew? "Even the part about you turning up naked in Cooper's bed?"

She had the decency to blush. "He told about that, huh?"

"He did."

"Wow, I was an idiot." She rubbed the bridge of her nose. "I don't know what else to say except I really do want to apologize. Because I am absolutely sorry. You don't have to forgive me. But I want you to at least know how sorry I am. And I own what I did. It was a terrible thing to do to you. And Cooper. And I was a terrible person to do it."

I narrowed my eyes. This was pretty convincing, but I'd developed a little cynicism lately. "Are you dying or something? Making amends so you can shuffle off this mortal coil with a clean conscience?"

She laughed. "No, nothing like that." She shrugged. "Just being adult, I guess. And if I get this job, I'll be in town again with my boyfriend—"

"You have a boyfriend? Good for you." That was nice. And it made her seem, I don't know…less likely to be trying to break anyone else up again.

"Yep. He's a great guy. Kind and sweet, and he dotes on me. Part fae, so we have pointy ears in common. And he's so good at all the backend stuff."

I stared at her. Um, *ew*. "I don't really need to know the details of your private life."

Her eyes widened, then she laughed and her face went bright red. "Okay, that did not come out the way I meant it. I mean that he sets up all my equipment, helps me do sound checks, runs the lighting, helps me plan the shows. Even makes sure I have water or snacks while I'm working. *That* backend stuff. Work stuff. He's really helped me take things to the next level."

21

"That's great." I meant that. Having that kind of support was invaluable. And I was super glad to hear she wasn't talking about their private sexy times.

"It is. He even encouraged me to talk to you and Cooper and make amends. And it would just be nice if when I come back to town, things aren't so…"

"Awkward?"

She nodded. "Yes. I don't expect us to be joined at the hip again. Or to double date or anything like that. Just for us to be civil. What do you say? Can we at least get to that place? I promise I have zero interest in Cooper. I'm completely committed to my guy. Have been for some time. Anyway, what do you think? Can we move past the past?"

I was about to answer when our food arrived.

When Mia dropped off the food and left, I was still searching for words. Lark's comments about being adult and moving beyond the past had struck home. I'd wanted her to know how different I was than the gullible, somewhat sheltered girl I'd been in college, and yet, I wasn't having very adult thoughts about forgiveness and moving on.

She spoke again before I could vocalize any of that. "Listen, you don't have to answer now. How about you think it over and text me in a day or so?"

Wow, she was really adult. I guess I should be too. Forgiving her and moving on *felt* like the right thing to do, I just wasn't completely there yet. "Thanks. That would give me a chance to get my head around all of this."

"Sure." She picked up her burger. "In the meantime, let's eat. Then I'll get out of your hair.

Dinner's on me, by the way. I can at least do that much."

"That's not nec—"

"Jayne, please." The sincerity in her eyes was unquestionable. "It's just dinner. Let me do this."

"Okay. Thanks." I grabbed my burger and dug in, but the food didn't have its usual flavor. That was all on me and my mood, not whoever was in the kitchen. I tried to get over myself. If Lark and I could have dinner together, maybe that was a sign that the past really was behind us.

"You seem happy." She picked up a fry. "I'm glad about that."

"I am. You seem happy too. The DJing going well?" I asked without thinking about it, but I guess I was sort of curious.

She grinned. "It is. I love my life. I am so much more successful than I ever thought I would be. I love the traveling and I love my job." She pointed the fry at me. "You know, being a DJ is its own kind of magic."

"How so?"

She laughed. "I keep people up all night. I keep them dancing and having fun. I control their entire evening with my choices. I can take a room from high energy to intense and intimate, then lift them right back up again. It's amazing."

This was the old Lark I knew. The one who would find something, fall in love with it, and make it her obsession until she'd mastered it. No wonder she'd become a success.

But all I could do was nod.

Why was I struggling with this so much? Why couldn't I be more adult? I thought about that while I chewed what really was a delicious burger. Maybe it was because her betrayal was relatively fresh to me. I'd only found out about it after coming to Nocturne Falls and having my heart-to-heart with Cooper, whereas it was old news to her. She'd been living with it for years.

Years. Almost eleven of them, to be exact. And yet, it was only because she'd realized we were going to be in the same town that she'd decided to apologize.

The food went tasteless again.

She was apologizing because my forgiveness would make her life easier. At least it seemed that way. My irritation returned, crawling up my spine until a chill settled over me.

"Hey." Lark laughed. "You're freezing me out over here."

When my attention refocused, I saw frost on our glasses. I made myself relax. Sometimes, when my emotions got the best of me, they spilled out in the forms of ice or snow. Or, obviously, frost. It was a winter elf thing.

My appetite was gone. Maybe in part because I was exhausted. I held up my hand and caught the eye of our server. She trotted over. "What can I do for you?"

"Can I get a box please?"

"Sure thing." She went off to fulfill my request.

I looked at Lark. "I'm sorry. It's been an exceptionally long day for me. I need time to process everything, but that's not going to happen tonight. It may not even happen tomorrow. All I can tell you is it's not going to happen until I'm rested and able to think clearly, so if you'll excuse me, I'm going to go home."

Mia dropped the box off.

I dumped my burger and fries into it, then closed the box.

Lark nodded sort of numbly. "Sure, okay…"

"Hey, it's not just you being here. I promise." I dug a twenty out of my purse and laid it next to my plate, then I stood. "I appreciate your offer to buy, but let's just go dutch. I'll call you as soon as I can."

"I—all right. Talk to you soon. Hope you get some rest."

I nodded, walked out, and kept going toward my apartment. I felt like I'd relived the whole betrayal all over again, and her sitting there, chatting about how great her life was now wasn't helping. Like I should just be okay with her waltzing in, saying she was sorry, then pretending like everything was perfect between us again. Like she shouldn't have to do any kind of penance for her bad behavior.

Well, I wasn't okay with it. And apparently, I wasn't that adult after all.

I was in the elevator when my phone rang. Cooper. I answered. "Hey."

"Hey yourself. You okay? You left sort of abruptly."

"Yeah, I'm fine. Totally beat and not really thinking clearly. Thanks for being there, though. I feel like we should forgive her and get over this, but that's my head talking. My heart isn't so sure."

"I get that."

I knew he would. "Anyway, I'm kinda done for the day. Can we talk more tomorrow?"

"Of course. Totally understand. Get some sleep. You've earned it."

"Thanks. You too."

"Night, Jay."

"Night, Coop." I let myself into my apartment. Relief at being home swept through me. I was so over being awake. I stuck the food in the fridge, brushed my teeth, stripped off my clothes, and pulled on an old T-shirt. I was too tired for full-on pajamas. And really, who would I be being cute for anyway?

I climbed into bed next to Spider, who hadn't moved since I'd left, and fell asleep before I pulled the covers up.

I woke up only because I'd forgotten to close the blinds and sunlight flooded the room with wretched enthusiasm. I blinked a few times and thought about how awesome it would be to still be asleep. But I had responsibilities, and today was not my day off.

Or was it? What day was it? I was too groggy to remember. I grabbed my phone off the nightstand and checked. Tuesday. Today was Tuesday. And it was seven eighteen.

Despite the blinding, early morning sun, I was surprised I hadn't slept later. I liked to be in the office by nine, which meant I could still sleep for at least another half an hour. I groaned and rolled back over.

But that noise and movement were all it took to alert the man of the house that I was awake. Spider jumped up onto the bed, walked over, and stood on me, staring down with the kind of intent that didn't need explaining.

He meowed anyway.

I smiled and scratched his chin. "Morning, sweets. Hungry?"

He leaned into the scritches, but it wasn't so good he couldn't answer. Not when breakfast was on the line. "Spider starving."

I dropped my hand and made a face at him. "You are not starving, I promise." I was guilty of not topping off his dry-food bowl before going to bed last night, though. "I'm getting up. But I can't do that with you standing on me."

He jumped down.

Somehow, I dragged myself to the kitchen. His bowl of dry food *was* empty. Clearly, I was a bad cat mother. "Sorry," I mumbled.

I refilled it with kibble, gave him fresh water, then a bowl of the thing that I knew would get me back into his good graces. His favorite canned food. Chicken Party.

If Purrfect Cat ever stopped making it, I was in serious trouble. "Here you go, Chicken Party."

He kneaded his front feet on the floor in a little dance, which was so cute it hurt. "Spider loves Chicken Party."

"So I've heard."

He made little happy noises while he ate, which lightened my mood considerably. If only my life were so easy. I thought about going back to bed, but if I did that, I wasn't going to have any desire to wake up again in half an hour.

Work beckoned. And don't get me wrong, I loved my job. Loved the people I worked with even more. But today I felt about as worky as a hundred-year-old ice sloth. Which is to say not at all.

My stomach growled, reminding me I hadn't really eaten dinner. But the leftover burger and fries were not going to cut it for breakfast. Today, of all days, I needed sugar. It's kind of a winter elf requirement to have a certain daily amount of sugar. Our high metabolisms can handle it, too, which is basically a superpower all on its own.

Sadly, I was out of doughnuts. I was out of a lot of things, but I didn't feel like getting dressed to go out to eat, even though a stack of Mummy's chocolate chip pancakes sounded like heaven right now.

Then the image of one of Mummy's huge, gooey cinnamon rolls appeared in my brain. My mouth watered and my stomach growled again.

Snowballs.

Reluctantly, I pulled on jeans, a T-shirt, and a hoodie. Today was all about easy and comfortable. I brushed my teeth, scraped my hair back into a ponytail, threw on a ballcap and sneakers, and grabbed my purse and keys. On the way down to the first floor, I texted Cooper.

Headed to Mummy's for breakfast. Meet me?

He didn't reply until I was a block away. *Sorry, just saw this. Already here.*

See you soon. I'm a couple minutes away.

I looked around when I got inside. The place was jumping, but then, breakfast was one of their most popular meals. Cooper waved from a seat at the counter. I liked a booth, but I liked food more and I was too hungry to be fussy. His navy Nocturne Falls Fire Department jacket was slung over the stool beside him. He picked it up and patted the upholstery. It might have been the only free seat in the house.

I joined him. "Thanks."

"You're welcome. And good morning." A few bites of an omelet and scattering of home fries were all that remained on his plate. "I already ordered you a coffee and a cinnamon bun. I hope that's okay."

So okay I almost wept. "Perfect. And good morning to you too."

They arrived seconds later by way of a server named Arty, whose slicked-back pompadour and rolled sleeves seemed more 1950's than hipster. He had a pinup girl tattooed on one forearm and a heart bearing the word Mother on the other. I liked him already.

"Heard you needed some sugar, sugar." He set the coffee and cinnamon bun in front of me.

"Yes. So much."

"Can I get you anything else?"

Cooper snorted.

I shot him a look. "Small stack of chocolate chip pancakes, side of bacon." I'd learned from Birdie Caruthers that a woman couldn't live on carbs alone. A little protein was a good thing.

Arty tapped his finger on the counter. "Coming right up."

As he headed off to put my order in, I added cream and sugar to my coffee. "Thanks, Coop. I really need this."

"Don't tell me you didn't sleep last night."

"I did, but…just not as long as I would have

liked." I took a long sip of the coffee. It was hot and strong, and I swear I could feel it kicking in.

He looked at me over the rim of his own cup. "You want to tell me about Lark?"

"Sure." I took a second to collect my thoughts. I was happy to have someone to talk to about the whole situation. Especially Cooper, who was such a big part of what had happened. "It boils down to she doesn't want things to be uncomfortable if she gets the DJ job and has to be in the same town with me. Or us, I guess."

He seemed to ponder that a moment. Then his expression darkened. "So…she apologized because it suited her needs and her timing."

I knew Coop would get it. "In a nutshell, yes."

He muttered an impolite word. "She hasn't changed."

I sighed. "I don't know. Maybe she's doing it on her timing, but she did still apologize. And she came here almost a year before she'll be back to DJ the ball."

By the fresh light of day, I was feeling a lot more forgiving toward Lark. Everyone deserved a second chance, right?

"I guess," Cooper said.

My pancakes arrived, gloriously golden brown and flecked with chunks of chocolate. Arty put the plate down, adding a small pitcher of syrup and a second plate that held my side order of bacon.

"What do you think? That gonna do it?" He jerked his thumb toward the kitchen. "I can always have them whip up another stack."

I laughed. This guy was going places. "No, this will do it. Thank you. Actually, you know what? I'll take another stack to go and a half-dozen cinnamon rolls too."

He grinned. "I like the cut of your jib, missy. I'll get right on that."

I had no clue what a jib was or how it was cut, but I picked up my fork, ready to dig in. "Thanks." I put the fork back down. I'd almost forgotten syrup. A heavy drizzle later and I was back in business. And back to the topic at hand. "So, anyway, Lark. She's waiting on an answer from me. And I'm going to tell her that…yes, we can be civil. I'm not completely over what she did, but then, we're not picking up where we left off or anything like that. It's just what I said. Being civil."

I cut a big hunk of pancake off with my fork and devoured it while I waited for Cooper to respond.

He shook his head. "You sure that's what you want to do?"

I chewed and thought. After I swallowed, I answered, "Everyone makes mistakes, Coop. Sure, hers was like a nine on the emotional Richter scale, but nobody died, nobody was maimed, and in the grand scheme of things, holding on to a grudge isn't healthy."

He frowned. "Yeah, you're right. I'm not feeling very forgiving, but I can be civil."

"She's got a boyfriend now, too, so I'm pretty sure you don't have to worry about another surprise naked visit from her. So, you know, there's that."

He laughed a little. "Good to know."

I felt better already. Mostly because the sugar had hit my bloodstream, giving me a slight euphoria that lifted my mood.

He checked his watch. "I hate to run, but I'm on duty in a few minutes. You're sure you want to tell her everything's behind us?"

I stared at my pancakes, hoping for an answer there. "I don't know if I'm going to tell her that, but I do know that I'm not going to stand in the way of her getting this job. If I even could."

"I'm sure you could. One carefully worded conversation with Elenora and Lark would be out."

"Well, I'm not going to do that." I wasn't going to keep someone from earning a living because she'd tried to steal my boyfriend once upon a time. "*That* would be petty."

He winked at me. "Look at you being all adult. And I agree. I might not be feeling it, but it's the right thing to do. See you later, babe."

"Later." The man was hot and smart and exactly what I'd needed this morning. I finished my breakfast in record time, including the cinnamon bun and the bacon, then got my to-go order, and paid, leaving a hefty tip for Arty. I might have to sit at the counter more often.

I headed back to my apartment to shower and get ready for the day. There wasn't a cloud in the sky, and it was shaping up to be a gorgeous fall day in Georgia. I made a mental note to open the blinds in the living room for Spider and crack the window a bit. He loved to look outside and sniff the fresh air.

After my shower, I did my hair and makeup, then opted for the most comfortable work clothes I had that still looked professional, just in case Lark dropped in again. Even so, I was jonesing for my yoga pants an hour after being at my desk. Work was piling up, what with all the Christmas inventory we were getting.

It was about to get real up in here. Real. Freaking. Busy.

I was eyeballs-deep in spreadsheets and inventory comparisons from years past when a knock on my office door shook me back to reality. A dark figure was visible through the frosted glass. A man.

It wasn't Lark. I called that a win. "Come in."

The door opened and a vampire, who wasn't Greyson, walked into my office.

Hugh Ellingham's smile was terse and closed-mouthed. He was not happy about this visit. My hackles went up. "Miss Frost. I'm sorry to interrupt. Do you have a moment?"

I stood and brushed off the cinnamon bun crumbs. (What? Pancakes didn't last forever.) "Of course, Hugh. And call me Jayne, please. We're certainly well enough acquainted for that."

He smiled and nodded. "Of course."

Hugh Ellingham was one of the three brothers who ran Nocturne Falls. Elenora was their grandmother. From what I understood, when they'd bought the town decades ago, it had been bankrupt and crumbling. The Ellingham family had changed all that, building it into what it was today, a thriving mecca for Halloween-loving tourists—and a haven for supernaturals of every imaginable variety.

They'd even orchestrated the bespelled waters that supplied the town and kept the tourists blissfully in the dark about, well, what was really in the dark.

"What brings you by?"

He shut the door and remained standing. He offered me a small box that I instantly recognized. "I brought you a little something from Delaney. Truffles. I hope you like them."

I snorted, unable to stop myself. "I don't think that will be a problem. Thank you." They were one of my favorite indulgences. "Please have a seat."

He nodded. "Very kind of you to let me interrupt your workday." He sat stiffly, like relaxing was impossible. And he still hadn't told me why he was here.

I tucked the box of truffles away in a desk drawer as I sat, then turned my chair to face him. "Something's troubling you."

I got a quick flash of a genuine smile, then it was gone. "Troubling might be too strong a word, but yes, there is something...concerning me."

I waited.

He sighed. "It's come to my grandmother's attention that you are acquainted with a woman she's considering hiring for next year's Black and Orange Ball. Lark Bramble."

I nodded, not sure where this was going. "I

know her. Pretty well, actually. Or I did. We were great friends in college but lost contact after that. Can I ask how your grandmother found out I know Lark?" If Lark was using me as a reference, that might help explain her need to make things right between us.

"Greyson stopped by to inquire about Lark's possible hiring, and Delaney asked how he knew Lark, and one thing led to another. I'm afraid Delaney questioned him until he had no choice but to reveal your past with Miss Bramble."

I laughed softly. "It's okay. I take it you know about what she did to Cooper and me then?"

"I do." He frowned. "Terrible thing for a friend to do to another friend."

"I agree."

"Then you'll understand why my brothers and I are concerned about Elenora hiring her. Is she trustworthy?"

I started to answer, then hesitated. "I don't know. I wish I could tell you more, but Lark and I have been out of touch since that whole mess in college. Yesterday was the first time I'd seen her in almost eleven years."

"I understand." His mouth tightened like he was frustrated. "I don't know why Elenora insists on a DJ for next year's ball. It's not like her at all."

"I was thinking the same thing. Obviously, I don't know her that well, but she seems more the orchestra type. A nice string quartet, that sort of setup."

"She is. But something's going on. She's been very secretive lately. And strangely…gleeful." He grunted. "Not that Elenora keeping secrets is so strange, but gleeful is not a word I believe I've ever used to describe my grandmother before."

"Does she always plan the ball this early? It's almost a year until the next one."

"She does, but she also uses most of the same vendors year after year. It's not like they'd dare book another event without making sure the date for the Black and Orange Ball was reserved for her. The DJ, though, that's new. She's also been talking about increased security. We've never had a problem at the ball, I assure you. But hiring the DJ must have been a detail she felt needed to be taken care of immediately."

"Makes sense." I rested my arm on the desk and rapped my fingers on it lightly. "I wish I could tell you more about Lark. I can say that what happened between us, happened a long time ago. I'd like to think she's a different person now." I really didn't want to stand in the way of her getting this job. "And from what I understand, she's a very successful DJ. I'm sure she wouldn't be if she was breaking commitments and letting clients down."

"True. All of her references have been stellar. We just didn't like what we heard about you and her. As you know, we are very protective of our citizens. If you or Cooper don't want Elenora to hire her—"

"No." I held my hands up. "I do not want to be the reason Lark isn't hired. If Elenora wants her, then by all means, Elenora should hire her. I've talked to Cooper about it too. I know he feels the same way."

"And you won't be bothered by her presence in town? Or at the ball? Because, naturally, the family hopes you'll attend."

I smiled. "I can't say I'm going to love having her in town, but I have a year to get used to the idea. And she'll be in her booth, or whatever DJs work out of, so it's not like I have to mingle with her."

Hugh stood. "Very true. Your attitude is commendable, Miss—Jayne. But then, I shouldn't be surprised by it. I know you were brought up with the grace and sensibility of royalty. Your good breeding shows."

"Thanks." I repressed a laugh as I got to my feet as well. "Hey, tell that to my parents next time they're in town, will you?"

He'd started for the door, then paused. "Say, do you think they'd like to come to the ball?"

"I don't know. I can ask. But the months before Christmas are unbelievably busy for them."

"I'm sure. But please extend them an invitation.

And I will make sure they receive a formal invite when those are sent out."

"I'll let them know."

He opened the door. "Thanks again for your time."

"Of course. And thank Delaney for the truffles for me."

"Absolutely." He left, closing the door behind him.

I sat down and got the box of truffles out. It's not like they'd stay fresh forever. It was my culinary duty to eat them, really. I opened the box and savored the delicious aroma of chocolate and sugar that wafted out. Then I picked the one that had a sliver of candied lemon rind on top and bit in. My taste buds did a little booty shake as the sweet tang of lemon and thyme and dark chocolate danced on my tongue.

Delaney might be a vampire, but what she did with chocolate and sugar could be considered witchcraft. It was supernaturally good. I finished the truffle, leaning back in my chair with my eyes closed to really enjoy how incredible it was.

A soft throaty laugh brought me upright again. "Am I interrupting something?"

I went upright immediately at the sound of that familiar Irish lilt. "Greyson, hi. No, I was just—"

"Eating chocolates?" His gaze went to the open box of truffles on my desk.

"Yes. Want one?"

"No, thanks."

I looked longingly at the one with a coffee bean and crystals of sea salt on top. No doubt a salted mocha caramel. "I need the sugar. It's all that's keeping me going."

He took up residence on the same love seat Hugh had just occupied. "I'm surprised you're here. Can't you take the day off?"

"I could. But then I'd just be even more backed up tomorrow. Christmas is right around the corner. This time of year is insane for us."

"I can imagine." His brow wrinkled. "Anything I can do to help?"

I thought for a minute. I was very willing to take him up on his offer, but nothing came to mind. "Not really. I'm getting two seasonal employees this year, and they show up next week, so I'll have plenty of help."

"And then will you take a day off?"

"I will. Oh! I know something you can do for me. If you really meant what you said about helping."

"I did. And I'll do it. What do you need?"

I smiled sweetly. "Could I talk you into grocery shopping for me? My cupboards are a little bare."

He laughed. "Yes, I can do that. Do you have a list?"

"Not yet, but I could put one together in a couple minutes."

He sat back and kicked his feet up on the small coffee table. "Go ahead. I'll wait."

I grabbed a steno pad and a pen and started writing. Chicken Party was at the top of the list. As was cat litter. And then doughnuts, both chocolate and powdered. Such were my priorities.

He crossed his arms behind his head, really making himself comfortable. "I should tell you that the Ellinghams know about your past with Lark." He sighed. "Delaney should work for the police as an interrogator."

"Hugh was here right before you were." I kept scribbling. *Two boxes mac-n-cheese. The kind with the sauce in the pouch. Four frozen pizzas. The ones with everything.*

Greyson put his feet on the floor and leaned forward. "And?"

One box each of Ho-Hos, Snowballs, and Ring Dings. Frozen waffles. Syrup. "And everything is fine. I'm not going to stand in the way of them hiring Lark. What she did to Cooper and me happened a decade ago, and it shouldn't have any bearing on her ability to do a good job at the ball."

"Huh."

I glanced over. "Does that surprise you? That I'm not out for revenge?"

"A little. But then again, not really. You're more level-headed than that."

"Very adult of me, right?" I went back to my list.

Doritos, Ruffles, large French onion dip. One bag baby carrots.

"Very."

Smiling, I added a few more things to the list, then handed it to him.

He read it, then looked at me. "Is this for real? I mean, I know you love sugar and eat like a teenage boy about to go through a growth spurt, but—"

"Hey, there are baby carrots on there."

Amusement bent his mouth. "Well, yes, that clearly balances out the vat of marshmallow fluff you've requested."

"Ooo, that reminds me. I need graham crackers too."

He stood, letting out a sound that was half laugh, half sigh. "I'll get them. How about I text you on the way back so you can meet me at your apartment and I can just carry everything in?"

I went to the door with him. "Sounds perfect. Very kind of you to do this for me."

He leaned in, his familiar scent of cinnamon filling my space. "Can't have my favorite girl starving to death, now can I?"

I smiled and kissed him on the mouth. A quick one. I wasn't looking to start anything while I was at work. "You're the best, thank you."

He sauntered out, the list clutched firmly in his hand. "Make sure you tell elf boy that."

Speaking of elf boy, I mean, Cooper, I needed to call him. Not to tell him Greyson was the best (I still wasn't anywhere close to deciding between them, and until they pushed me, I was happy with how things were), but to explain that I'd essentially given the Ellinghams the go-ahead to hire Lark.

I felt good about that. It was proof I was moving on. And while I hadn't exactly vouched for Lark, I certainly hadn't gotten in her way. I almost hoped she got the job. Was that weird? Maybe. I hoped Cooper would feel the same way. But I also understood he had harder feelings about the whole thing than I did.

He picked up as soon as I called, and I gave him the rundown on my conversation with Hugh.

"So that's it, then," he said. "She'll be at the ball."

The tone of his voice said it all. Resignation. Disappointment. And a little resentment. I sighed.

"Are you mad at me? What else could I do? This is her livelihood. It wouldn't be fair of me to get in the way of that."

"No, you're absolutely right. And I'm not at all mad at you. You did the right thing. This is my issue to get over. And I will. But hey, what does it matter? She'll be there working, and we'll be there to have fun."

"Yes, exactly." I smiled. I knew Cooper would come to terms with it.

"Does this mean you've forgiven her?"

"I don't know. Not entirely. But I'm starting to get over it. Look, I can't carry this weight for the rest of my life. That's not healthy. And you and I are friends again now. That has to count for something."

"True." The resentment was gone, but a new longing filled his voice. "But if not for her interference, I can't help but think you and I would be a lot further along in our relationship by now."

I had no doubt he was right. In the future that never happened, we most likely would have been married and probably would have had some kids by now. A new, small ache opened up in my heart. "I'm so sorry, Coop," I whispered. I felt for him. I cared for him deeply. And part of me very much regretted all that hadn't happened between us.

But did I wish that I was his wife? That wasn't a question I could easily answer. My life was so different now than it had been back when I thought marriage was the direction we'd been headed.

I'd practically counted on it. Even bought a few of those enormous bride magazines. Then Lark had happened. Now, my future—or at least the man in it—was no longer clear.

He sighed. "You're right. I need to get over this too. It's just going to take me some time. Don't expect me to be chummy with her. It's never going to happen."

"I'm fine with that. I don't see her and me braiding each other's hair or swapping clothes any time soon. But to be civil at the ball? By next October, I should be able to swing that. And so should you."

A grunt answered me. "I'll let you know next October."

"Fair enough." He'd get over this soon enough. And I could humor him until that happened. "Hey, you want to get pizza tonight?"

"I can't. I'm on shift for the next four nights."

"I could get some pies and bring them to the station." I was still worn out and not completely up for that, but if it would help Cooper's mood, which it would, I was all in.

"That's a nice offer, but you're tired. Get some rest, babe."

"Okay. But call me if you change your mind."

He laughed, a sound that lifted my own mood.

"I won't. You need your sleep. But I love your determination. Later, babe."

"Later." We hung up, and while we'd ended on a happier note, I couldn't help but feel that things seemed a bit off between us. Had Lark's reappearance caused a new rift? Maybe I was reading too deeply into it. Or maybe I was right.

Only time would tell.

October (current month)

In the eleven months that had passed since Lark had first shown up (and thankfully, left again), life had pretty much gone back to normal. We survived the Christmas rush. I dated Cooper. I dated Greyson. I worked, hung out with Juni and Buttercup, talked to my parents, loved on Spider, ate way too much sugar, you know, all the regular stuff.

It was absolutely life as usual.

And I had thought eleven months would be plenty of time for Cooper to mellow out about Lark's transgressions against us.

I was right. Even after she texted both of us a week after leaving to say she'd gotten the job of DJing the ball and how thankful she was that we hadn't let the past affect her future. Or something like that.

Sure, we'd gone out that night and overindulged in some Salvatore's pizza and shared a massive sundae at I Scream, but we'd made peace with the fact that Lark was going to be at the ball with us. Working, obviously, but at the ball.

Cooper and I had matured. And we were pretty proud of ourselves. The invites had come for the ball, and we (Greyson included) had RSVP'd that we'd be there. Ice was this year's theme, which seemed to jive with Lark's hiring.

Even so, ice was a slightly left of center theme for a masked Halloween ball, but hey, it was Elenora's party and she was footing the bill. She could have made the theme zombie Muppets for all people cared.

Cooper had decided to go as a melted snowman, which I thought was hilarious. (And based on his decision that *melted snowman* also meant *shirtless*, I thought it might be his way of showing Lark what she wasn't getting.) Greyson was leaning toward frost giant, which apparently also involved shirtlessness. And blue body paint and a fur kilt.

No complaints.

Seeing as how I was already the Winter Princess, I was going as myself. Yeah, I know. Not very imaginative. But it was a chance for me to wear my snowflake tiara and my court gown. It was very pretty. Ice blue silk covered in hand-beaded silver snowflakes and edged in crystalline frost lace. Also, it had this high, stand-up collar that framed my face in a kind of fairy-tale way.

Completely over the top, but also utterly fabulous. And since my parents had decided things were too busy with Christmas prep for them to attend (as suspected), it was up to me to represent the North Pole in all its sparkly, frozen glory.

Life was good when the biggest burden you had to bear was wearing a custom-made gown and a ransom in jewels in the name of fun.

Based on past experience, I probably should have worried that things couldn't stay smooth for long. But I pushed those thoughts aside to give my full attention to the gooey cheesesteak subs Cooper and I were devouring at Howler's. "C'mon, Coop. I know you don't like sharing the evening with Greyson, but you guys have got to figure out if you're going to split the evening or try for a full-on three-way date the entire evening. I realize the ball is still ten days away, but I'd like to know what you guys want to do now."

He laughed as he ate his last fry. "I am *not* having a three-way with fang face."

"You know what I mean."

He winked. "Yeah, I do. As much as I'd like to have you to myself for a few hours, I'm too curious about Lark to want to leave the party. I'd rather be there all night."

"Okay, I'll let Greyson know."

"He's not going to like that."

"He's going to be fine with it, and you don't care anyway, so hush." I laughed.

"Well, you won't be the only one there with two dates."

"No? Who else?"

Coop snorted. "Who do you think? Birdie. And my boss is one of them."

"Hah! Yeah, that makes sense. It's also very sweet." Birdie Caruthers was aunt to Titus, the fire chief; Hank, his brother and the sheriff; and their sister, Bridget, the lovely owner of this fine establishment. The Merrows were a swell bunch. The nicest (and only) werewolves I'd ever known. Maybe Birdie was taking both her nephews. Titus was single, and Hank was married, but Hank and his wife had a baby at home. She might be staying in with the little one.

"It is sweet. Although the chief told me Jack Van Zant also asked her."

"Remind me who that is again?" I took a big bite of my sub while he answered.

"Cole Van Zant's dad. Pandora's future father-in-law."

I nodded as I swallowed. "Why didn't Birdie want to go with him?"

Cooper smirked. "She did. That is, she is. Jack is her second date. Apparently, she's been hanging out with you too much, because she decided that she wanted to go with her nephew but also dance with Jack. So there you have it."

I rolled my lips in. That did sound like something she might have picked up from me, but then again, Birdie wasn't known for her restraint or inhibitions.

He leaned in, his face suddenly more serious. "I do hope Lark doesn't do anything stupid."

"Like what?"

"I don't know, but it's Lark. She'll probably try to make small talk. Or something."

"Maybe, but she won't really be around to do that for the most part. She'll be in her DJ booth."

He frowned. "No, she won't. I looked her up on YouTube. She walks through the crowd a lot at her shows."

"How is that possible?"

"She has a control panel about the size of an iPad. She can run her entire show off that, from what I've seen."

Snowballs. I wasn't really interested in getting chatty with her.

Cooper's phone rang. He glanced down at the screen. He was on call, so the phone on the table was excusable. (The fact that he was sitting across from me in his uniform looking super hot more than made up for it.) He glanced at the screen and made a strange face.

"The station?"

He picked up the phone. "No. My dad." He answered. "Hey, Dad, what's up?"

I ate a few fries and tried to figure out if I was eavesdropping or not, but decided if Cooper needed privacy, he'd probably go outside.

"Since when? Yes. Of course. Take her anyway. Now. Let me know." Cooper hung up. "My mom's not feeling well. Having a hard time maintaining her temperature. My dad thinks it could be minor heatstroke, but she doesn't want to go to the doctor. She's pretty stubborn."

"Oh, Cooper." Heatstroke for a summer elf was the equivalent of a heart attack in a human. Or hypothermia in a winter elf. The body went haywire and stopped processing temperature the way it was supposed to. It generally didn't happen until a person was older, but sometimes there wasn't any real explanation either. "Is she okay?"

He shook his head, the pain in his eyes easily readable. "She says she is, but like my dad said, she won't go to the doctor. He thinks if I come down there, I can talk her into it."

"You have to go. You're going, right?" My heart was breaking for him.

"We'll see. My dad's going to try to get her to the doctor one more time. If he can't, I'll head down."

"They're in Florida, right?"

He nodded distractedly. "Boca."

"You should go, Coop. I mean, leave here and go to the station and tell Titus what's going on and that you might need time off."

He blinked and seemed to come back to me. "Yeah, that's not a bad idea." He threw his napkin on the table.

"What can I do to help? I could help you pack or make your travel arrangements or—"

"Not yet." He smiled quickly. It didn't reach his eyes, but it had been for my benefit. "I can handle it if it comes to that. Thank you, though."

"She's going to be all right. You'll see." I reached out and grabbed his hand. "Hey, I can come with you, if you want."

"I don't even know if I'm going yet." He smiled a little more. "And that's sweet, babe, but you have the store to run and the ball to go to. And one of us needs to be there. Otherwise, Lark will think we decided not to be adult."

I laughed softly. "Yeah, I thought about that."

"And you still offered to go with me?" He squeezed my hand. "Thanks."

I shrugged. "You said yourself you don't like the idea of me and Greyson alone for the evening."

He blew out a breath. "I don't. But you and I have something you and he will never have."

I raised my brows in question.

"*We* have history."

"True."

He let go of my hand and grabbed his phone. "All right, I better go square things with the chief. Don't worry about the bill. I already told Bridget to put it on my tab."

"Thanks. Please keep me posted about your mom when you can."

"I will." He got up and kissed my cheek. "See you later."

I held on to his arm for a moment. "She's going to be okay."

"Thanks." He headed for the door.

"Princess Jayne!" Birdie's effusive tone echoed through the restaurant.

Cooper was a few steps away. He turned back to me. "There you go, now you won't have to finish your lunch alone."

Birdie sidled up to him, giving him these big moony eyes. "Well, well, how's the hottest fireman in town?"

"I'm good, Birdie." He gave her a big smile. How he managed that with the news about his mom weighing on him, I had no idea, but Cooper was that kind of guy. Never wanted anyone to worry about him. "You look lovely as always."

She clutched at nonexistent pearls. "Thank you, sweetheart. Are you leaving?"

"Yep. Have to head to the station. But you're welcome to take my seat and keep Jayne company while she finishes her lunch."

"Perfect. You have a good day now."

"You too." He gave me a quick, sad smile and left.

Birdie slid into his seat. "What's that look on your face?"

I stopped staring after Cooper to face her. "Cooper's mom is having some health issues. He might have to head out of town to see her, depending on how things go."

"That poor man! He didn't say a word."

I shrugged. "That's just how he is."

Bridget walked up to the table. "Hi, Aunt Birdie." She leaned in and kissed Birdie's cheek.

"Hi, darling."

"You in for lunch?"

"No, just cobbler and a sweet tea."

"Ice cream?"

Birdie frowned. "Is there any other way?"

"It was silly to ask." Bridget glanced at me. "And I'll bring you a fresh Dr Pepper."

"Thanks." Mine was only half gone, but I wasn't going to argue.

As soon as Bridget left, Birdie scooted forward. "I'm very sorry about Cooper's mother, but I have news of my own. News you need to know."

"What?" Birdie was a better source of info than the internet.

Her brows lifted conspiratorially. "She's here."

I looked around. "Who's here?"

"Your arch-nemesis. The bird woman."

I felt like I should know this one, but I didn't. "Who?"

"Lark," Birdie hissed through clenched teeth.

Oh, *that* bird woman. I stared at her. "Lark is in town?"

Birdie nodded so furiously I thought her earrings might come off.

"Why? It's so early." The ball was a week and a half away. Why did Lark need to be here already? I took another bite of my cheesesteak and pondered this new development.

Birdie shrugged. "Beats me, but she's here." She waggled her head back and forth. "Her and her *lover*, Lance."

I almost snorted grilled onions through my nose. I swallowed and found some composure. "Lance? How do you know he's her lover?" Not that I doubted Birdie. The woman was a font of information. And Lark had mentioned a boyfriend when we'd had dinner last year.

Birdie sat back, obviously pleased with herself. "I could tell just from the way they interacted. Also, they had to come in and get their temporary business license at the sheriff's department. They both listed the same rental property address here in town. So there's that."

"Huh. I guess it makes sense that she brought her boyfriend. She said something about him being her assistant, but to be honest, I didn't pay that much attention.

"He's not just her boyfriend. He's also her—"

"Here you go, ladies." Bridget came over with our drinks in one hand and a ridiculously large piece of peach cobbler for Birdie in the other. It was matched in size only by the half gallon of vanilla bean ice cream melting over it.

Then I noticed there were two spoons.

She set the cobbler down in front of Birdie, along with the sweet tea. "You share that with Jayne, now. I brought two spoons. There's more than enough. I know you like to overindulge, but—"

"Ahem." Birdie cut her eyes at Bridget. "Don't be sassy with me, sassmouth. I changed your diapers, missy." Then she put on a sugary smile. "But I would be happy to share with the princess."

I'd long ago given up trying to get her to just call me Jayne. I grinned at Bridget. "That was really nice of you."

She picked up my old soda glass. "No problem. Y'all enjoy."

I leaned in as she walked away. "He's also what? What were you going to say?"

"Hmm?" Birdie hoisted a spoonful of cobbler and ice cream that could have choked a yeti.

"Lark's boyfriend. You said he wasn't just her boyfriend."

"Oh, right, yes." She ate the cobbler first. Naturally. The woman's appetite occasionally put mine to shame. She finally swallowed. "He's like her roadie or something. He sets up her equipment, runs the lights, makes sure she's got what she needs while she's working. That sort of thing."

"Oh, yeah, she told me about this guy when we had dinner the first time she showed up here. So, Lark and Lance. How about that?" I stuffed the last bite of my cheesesteak into my mouth so I could finish it quickly. I had to, or the cobbler would be gone.

Birdie pursed her lips. "Lance LaFlame, to be exact."

I managed not to choke on my food and swallowed. "That has to be a stage name. Please tell me that's a stage name."

"Beats me. That's what he used to register."

My phone chimed. I dug into my purse for it. "Sorry, I don't mean to be rude, but I have to check my messages in case there's a problem at the store."

Birdie waved my words away. "You go right ahead, honey."

I looked at the screen. It was a text from Greyson.

You around?

At Howler's.

Okay. Going to swing by in a few.

Okay. I put the phone away. Not sure what was up, but he'd explain when he got here. I picked up the second spoon. "Nice to see you saved me some cobbler. Now, tell me all about Jack Van Zant."

Her coy smile said volumes. "He's a nice man."

"Where did you meet him?" I dug in, scooping out a good mouthful of biscuit crust, warm peaches, and melted ice cream.

"I just…ran into him in town."

She was being oddly secretive. "Have you been out on a date already?"

"I don't know if you could really call it a date."

I gave her a sly look. "Then what would you call it?"

"Well—"

"Jayne."

We both looked up to see Greyson stalking toward us. His whole body looked tense, and his eyes held clear frustration.

Birdie made a small sound of pleasure. I was about to make a comment when I realized it was because she'd eaten another bite of cobbler, not because she was crushing on my favorite vampire.

I went back to him. "Hey, Greyson. What's up?"

Frowning, he shook his head. "I have bad news."

"Oh no, what happened?"

Birdie put her spoon down. "You all right, son?"

He nodded at her. "I'm fine, Birdie. Just not happy."

"Sit," I said. "Tell us what's going on."

He shook his head again. "I can't. I'm on my way to the airport."

Birdie put her hand to her throat. "There was a death, wasn't there?"

"No," he said. "But death is involved." He sighed. "I have to go to Rome for Lucian."

I lifted one shoulder. "That doesn't sound so bad."

"I will be there until October 31st."

My stomach clenched. "But you'll be home for the ball, right?"

He sighed. "At best, I might make the last hour. But most likely, I won't."

"Son of a nutcracker." And just like that, I went from two dates to none.

Anger sparked in his eyes. "I'm very sorry to break our date. And even sorrier that elf boy will have you to himself."

"Yeah, about that. Cooper's probably not going. He just found out his mother is having some health issues and needs him to be with her."

"I hope she'll be okay." Then Greyson sighed. "Now I feel worse knowing you'll be all alone at the ball."

"I'll be fine."

"I know you will. But I still feel bad about canceling on you. Although slightly better knowing that old pointy ears won't be the beneficiary of my cancellation."

I tucked a strand of hair behind my own pointed ear. "You had better bring me something amazing from Italy."

He grinned. "Of course." Then he moved in and kissed me on the mouth. "Thank you for being so understanding. I'm off to the airport."

"Bye. Travel safe." Two in one day. What were the odds?

Birdie waved as he left, then returned to the cobbler. "So, all alone for the Black and Orange Ball."

"Apparently," I muttered. I stabbed my spoon into the cobbler and was having thoughts about ordering a second one.

She tipped her head, her smile widening. "I can fix that."

"That's very kind of you, but I'm not interested in taking either of your dates away from you." Titus was a very handsome man, but he was also Cooper's boss. That would be weird. And Jack had to be Birdie's age. He was probably a charming fellow, but I wasn't into the older-man thing. At least not that much older.

"Pssh." Her forehead crinkled. "I'm not giving you either one of them. Not that Titus isn't a lovely man. He is. My nephew is a fabulous catch. And handsome as all get-out. But he's the fire chief and Cooper's a fireman, and well..." She shrugged. "You know."

"Right," I said around a mouthful of peaches. "And Jack's not exactly my demographic."

"No, he is not." Her smile returned. "But I have someone else in mind."

"Who?"

She shook her finger at me. "Let me work my magic first. No point in getting your hopes up."

"I can't get my hopes up for a man I know nothing about. And I'm not sure I want to be fixed up on a blind date."

"How about if it's not blind? You could meet him ahead of time. See if you like him or not. I can make that happen without telling him you're looking for a date. Let me feel him out first and see if he's open to it. Or even available to attend the ball."

"I don't know…" I was a little too bummed about both my guys being off the roster to think about anyone else just yet. I couldn't help but be worried about Cooper's mom, too. I loved my mom dearly. If anything happened to her, I'd be a mess.

Birdie patted my hand. "Life can really be a bother sometimes, can't it?"

"You can say that again." I sighed. "Maybe I'll just go stag."

Birdie clucked her tongue. "After telling Lark you were dating two men? How's that going to look?"

"Snowballs. Dirty, yellow snowballs." I groaned. "I guess I better have a date. Who is this guy? Please tell me he's not some dweeb who's already been turned down by every other woman in town."

Her eyes sparkled with a joyful, but slightly

naughty, light. "I think you're going to like him very much. For more than a couple of reasons."

"That doesn't tell me who he is. Have I already met him?" I tried to think about all the single men in town I knew. Which weren't that many. "It's not Pete the pharmacist, is it? Because he and Juniper are a thing, you know. I don't want to be the reason anyone else loses a date."

"I wouldn't do that."

I pushed a hunk of biscuit topping around with my spoon. "I know. I'm just...not happy."

"Of course you're not, honey. It's a terrible blow to lose both your beaus. And I'm sure you're worried about both of them. Well, about Cooper's mother. And who knows what Lucian has sent Greyson to Rome for! But Birdie's on the case. I am very mindful of the kind of man a woman of your status needs. I'm not going to fix the Winter Princess up with any old crumb bum." She nodded at me. "Have faith."

"All right, I will." I made a halfhearted attempt at a smile. "Thanks." But deep down, I couldn't see myself having fun at the ball with anyone but Coop or Greyson. Birdie's pick better be stellar, or chances were good that I'd turn him down.

No matter what Lark might think about me showing up solo, because who cared what Lark thought? Except me. A little.

Lunch had gone on long enough, so I said my

goodbyes and made my way back to the office. It was a Wednesday, and Christmas was approaching fast, which meant there would be new inventory coming through the Santa's Bag.

Every Santa's Workshop store had one. It was our magical way of transporting goods from the North Pole to the shops. The bag was one of the most magical creations to come out of the NP, and also the most secret. Especially because it was basically a direct portal from the NP to wherever the bag was.

Almost anything could be sent through it, so long as it wasn't alive. This wasn't a Beam Me Up, Scotty type of contraption, it was based on the original Santa's Bag. The one that belonged to my uncle. Which was also how it got its name. How else did you think he delivered all those toys to all those houses? After every couple of stops, the bag got magically refilled.

I walked into the warehouse and straight to the red velvet bag. It was bulging with new goodies, as suspected.

From there, I made a beeline into the shop to let Kip and Juniper know that I was back from lunch and to get Kip started on unloading the new goods, then I went into my office to see if there were any emails or other business I needed to take care of.

A knock made me look up. "Boss, package for you."

It was Kip. "Bring it in," I answered.

Kip came in holding a manila envelope and a box. The envelope most likely held the new inventory manifest. Electronics didn't work so well in the North Pole, so we still did a lot by hand. The box had my name scrawled on it in my mom's handwriting. I grinned as I stood up. That probably held goodies. Sweet, sugary goodies.

He handed them over. "Here you go, boss."

"Thanks." I took both from him. "What was in the shipment?"

"It's all Pocket Pets and a big display for them. I guess those are going to be the hot toy this year, huh?"

I nodded. "If we're getting tons of them, you can brace yourself for the insanity." I made a mental note to ask Birdie which one her grand-nephew Charlie would most like to have and set it aside for her.

"Where do you want me to put the display?"

"How big is it?"

"I haven't put it together yet, but I'd say it's a floor stand."

I thought about that. "Back of the store. Then people have to walk all the way through. We could pick up some impulse buys that way. But make sure you put a few by the register, too."

"You got it." He closed my door.

I sat down to open the envelope. Work first,

then the box of goodies. It would be my reward. I pulled the papers out and started going through them. Most of it was inventory sheets, but there was also the annual write-up on the coming Christmas season, which for the winter elves in the North Pole started February 1st, but for those of us working the stores, officially got under way the day after Halloween. Which was right around the corner.

The write-up, always done by my uncle, was filled with the usual holiday cheer and encouragement to make this our best Yule yet. I smiled as I read it, hearing the words in his warm, booming voice.

But I'd be lying if it also didn't make me a little homesick. I wondered if my mom knew that would happen and that's why she sent the box. She was pretty amazing like that. I set the paperwork aside as thoughts of home and family tugged at me. I could do the inventories later.

Right now, the box beckoned. I sliced my letter opener through the packing tape. The instant I did, the most delicious aromas rose up to meet me. Cinnamon, sugar, butterscotch, nutmeg, orange, and some other spices I wasn't sure about, but they were nostalgic scents that brought to mind the holidays and family and happy, comforting feelings.

My mouth was watering like mad as I pulled

out the note on top. It was affixed to a heavy, rectangular white paper box.

Just a few things from your aunt and me to remind you of home. We tried some new recipes. Hope you like them. Love you, honey. – Mom

P.S. Dad sent you a second snow globe for your office.

"Love you too, Mom." My heart was as warm and gooey as the peach cobbler I'd eaten earlier. I opened the new snow globe first, setting it on my desk. I realized this made me easier to get ahold of now, but I was good with that. Family was important.

Next, I dove into the rest of the big box. There were a bunch of various-sized plastic food containers inside. I took the first one out. I could tell it was snickerdoodles from the shapes visible through the plastic. I pried open the red lid and inhaled. The aroma told me instantly this was one of the new recipes. Cinnamon I expected, but orange too? This was going to be good.

I sealed that container and was about to open another one when someone knocked on my door.

Probably Kip with a report on the new stuff. I yelled, "Come in," without looking.

"Miss Frost?"

Not a voice I knew. I glanced up. "Oh, hi."

Oh wow. A very handsome, silvery-haired man had just walked into my office. And he was cradling a large pastry box in one well-muscled arm. *Large*. Like carry-on suitcase sized. "I mean, yes. I'm Jayne Frost."

He stuck a hand out. And grinned. I was temporarily mute. "Sinclair Crowe. It's a pleasure to meet you. I hope I'm not interrupting anything. You look awfully busy."

Wow, he had pretty eyes. Wait. What had he said? "Um, no, I'm not...I mean, I *am* busy, but you're good. I mean, you're not interrupting." Oh great, he was going to think this was a pity job given to me because I was addle-brained. I put the box of goodies from my mom into the desk drawer reserved for snacks.

I made myself straighten up and tried not to be so muddled by his hotness. I was around two very hot guys all the time. I should be practically immune to this degree of male sexiness by now. "You'll have to excuse me, my mind was elsewhere and I thought you were someone else coming in. I didn't know I was getting a visitor."

"I'm sorry. Do you want me to go?"

Um, NO. "No, please. You're fine." Literally. "What can I do for you, Mr. Crowe?"

"Sinclair, please. Or Sin. I answer to either."

A tall, handsome, sexy man who answered to Sin. I wasn't in trouble at all.

He went on. "I understand that you're a great connoisseur of sweets. So..." He put the box front

71

and center. "I brought you an offering. I'm sort of new to town and trying to get the word out about my business."

I looked closer at the top of the box. A well-decayed but cute zombie smiled up at me. His crumbling grin sat in the middle of the store name above and the slogan below that read *Better than brains*. "You own Zombie Donuts?"

"Yes." He held the box out toward me. "And I brought you some as a way of introducing myself. They should still be warm."

So handsome, nicely built, *and* he owned a doughnut shop. I started to think there might be a hidden camera somewhere. Could this guy be real? Or were my employees pranking me?

Pranks had kind of become a thing ever since the tinkers had sent a new prototype toy for the store. It looked like a box of chocolates, but when you opened it, foam poured out and filled the room. The foam only lasted for thirty seconds, but Buttercup had been sure I'd set her up.

My skepticism about Mr. Crowe must have shown on my face, because he pushed the box toward me a little more and opened the lid. "Go ahead, try one."

I gasped. I'd never seen such a decadent display. Now, I like doughnuts a lot. Probably more than your average individual, but I don't tend to be that picky. Give me a round of fried dough with icing on it and I'm a happy camper. Even better if it's been filled, but again, not that picky.

But these? These little masterpieces were next level. Brilliant, unusual colors. Candy decorations. Frostings and fillings that begged to be tasted. And the aroma? Like unicorns had learned to bake.

It would be impolite not to try one. I picked one that had a wide swathe of white icing decorated with a thick red cross. Looked sort of medical, which was kind of odd for a doughnut, but there were red and white sugar sprinkles on it too. That made it seem a little Christmasy and that appealed to me. Plus, it was clearly a filled doughnut, judging from the round shape, bulging fatness and little rosette of berry-colored cream on the side.

I looked at the one I'd picked, then at Mr. Crowe. I had to check one more time that this wasn't a prank. "This is a real doughnut, right? It's not like one of those ear wax jellybeans you think are actually vanilla, is it? Am I going to bite into this and get a mouthful of ketchup and hot sauce?"

He laughed, a deep, warm sound that seemed utterly genuine. "It's a real doughnut. I promise. That's actually one of my personal favorites. It's our Dr Prepper. You know, prepper like prepping for the apocalypse. Anyway, it's got vanilla and cherry frosting, and it's filled with Dr Pepper-flavored mousse."

I stared at him. "Dr Pepper."

He nodded. "Do you not like Dr Pepper? You can put it back and try another one. I brought them for you, after all."

Dr-freaking-Pepper. I was definitely being pranked.

I gave the whole thing two more seconds of thought. If I was being pranked, it was the best one yet. Might as well find out for sure. I took a big bite of the doughnut.

Can you die from pleasure? The answer was no, because if you could, that doughnut would have killed me. My extremities went numb for a moment with the amazingness of it. I closed my eyes, leaned against my desk, and basked in the sheer, sugary, Dr Peppery deliciousness coursing through me.

Only Sinclair's laughter brought me back to reality. "That is so cool."

I opened my eyes. Snowflakes drifted down from the ceiling in my office. I shut that right off. "Sorry about that. It's a perfectly natural winter elf reaction to high levels of emotion."

He frowned. "High levels of emotion?"

"I'm a winter elf. And your doughnut kind of

made me bliss out." I sighed and put the rest of the doughnut on a tissue on my desk for later. I would have rather shoved the whole thing in my mouth, but I was the Winter Princess after all. Winter Princesses didn't shove entire doughnuts into their mouths in front of strangers. Sadly. "I have a serious thing for sweets. And doughnuts. And especially Dr Pepper." Like he didn't know.

"Oh, right. Got it." His brows shot up. "I've never had anyone respond to one of my creations like that before. That was very, uh, impressive." His smile took on a sly bend. "I should have stopped by sooner."

"What made you stop by today?" For the briefest moment, I thought Birdie might have sent him, but he'd arrived too soon after our lunch to be the guy she hoped to set me up with. It had to be Buttercup. Or Juniper. Or all of them.

He shrugged. "If I'm being honest, I meant to come sooner, but I was a little intimidated by you."

Not this again. Instead of rolling my eyes, I reminded myself that, for some people, royalty was a big deal. "Look, I might be a princess, but I put my pants on the same way as everybody else."

He studied me for a long second. "You're a princess?"

"Isn't that why you were intimidated by me?"

He shook his head. "No. I was intimidated

because word on the street is you're a top consumer of sweets in this town, and I was afraid if you hated my doughnuts, it could be bad for business."

That couldn't be true, could it? Did people really consider me that much of a sugar hound?

He peered at me. "Are you really a princess?"

There was no point in denying it. "Yes. I'm the Winter Princess. Heir to the Winter Throne."

He mulled that over. "That would make your father...Jack Frost?"

I nodded. "You know your North Pole royalty."

"I like to keep up with the supernatural community. And since we're sharing, I should tell you I'm a necromancer. You'll probably hear people whispering about it anyway, but I don't go around broadcasting it because then people come looking for favors. And frankly, I rarely want to do them. Those kinds of favors tend to be pretty morbid. No pun intended. But yes, what they say about me is true."

"A necromancer? I don't really know what that is." Although he was right about the rumors. I had heard that. From Birdie, I think. "Something to do with dead people, right?"

"Right. I can see ghosts when others can't. I can talk to dead people. I can temporarily bring dead things back to life. I have a few other skills, but that sums up the big ones."

"Get out. That's pretty cool. And a little creepy."

He shrugged. "It's a blessing and a curse." He glanced down at the box still in his hands. "So...do you want these or should I take them back?"

I grabbed the box. Gently. As gently as you might expect me to take possession of a box filled with delicious works of art that tasted like everything that was right in the world and that I suddenly thought might be taken away from me. "Oh no, you brought these for me. They're staying right here."

He laughed as he let go. "Okay, good. That was their intended purpose."

"I'll probably share them with my employees." Provided this didn't turn out to be a prank. "And don't worry, I'll be happy to tell everyone I know about how great these are. I'll have to come by your shop. I've been meaning to since I heard about it. Just, you know, life."

"Yeah, I get that. It's hard running your own business. You're responsible for everything. On call constantly. It's tough. But your shop is great. You are obviously doing an outstanding job here."

"Thank you. That's really kind." It was nice to talk to someone who got it. "Hey, strange question, but my employees didn't set you up to come here, did they?"

"Nope. Definitely not. Although the one at the register did let me back here and tell me where your office was. Can I ask why you'd think that?"

No reason not to tell him. "Pranks have kind of become a thing around here lately. And to send a really hot guy into my office with a Dr Pepper-flavored doughnut the day both my dates to the Black and Orange Ball find out they can't go, well, it seemed like I was getting set up for something."

His brows shot up as a new warmth filled his gaze. "You had two dates and both of them canceled on you?"

"Yes. Both for good reasons, but it does make me sound pretty pathetic."

"Pathetic is the last word I'd use to describe you." His jaw shifted to one side, and he stuck his hands into the pockets of his jeans. "You know…I'd be happy to escort you to the ball. I mean, if you're interested in going with a guy who makes Dr Pepper-flavored doughnuts for a living and the whole communicating with the dead thing doesn't turn you off."

I smiled a big, dumb smile. Probably looked like I'd just been shot up with Novocain. And I'm 99 percent sure I blushed. Sinclair was asking me out. At least I think that's what was happening.

"I'd love to. If you don't mind going with a woman who can freeze you into a solid hunk of ice in under two seconds." I liked to let people know up front who they were dealing with. Especially men. Never hurt for them to have a little fear of you, I figured.

He shrugged. "All I heard is you just called me a hunk."

I laughed. "I like you, Sinclair."

"I like you too, Jayne." He took his hands out of his pockets. "I guess we should exchange numbers."

"Yes. But in all seriousness, I have to tell you that I've got some baggage that might be on display at the ball. I hesitate to tell you this, because I really don't want to go alone, but an old frenemy of mine is DJing the bash. I don't think anything will happen, but then again, who knows?"

"Ex-boyfriend?" He got his phone out.

"Old college roommate who caused my boyfriend and me to break up, then tried to seduce him for herself."

His eyes widened. "How about that. And you're still talking to this woman?"

"Not really. But we've agreed to be civil."

He pondered that. "We should probably go to dinner so you can tell me everything in detail. You know, prep me for the big night. And we can get to know each other better that way."

I smiled. He'd just asked me out again. And why not? "Okay. Tomorrow night?" Tonight was movie night with the girls.

"Anyplace special you want to go?"

"Anywhere but Claude's." Going there with

another guy would be awkward since that was kind of my spot with Greyson.

"How about that pub in town? The Poisoned Apple?"

"Sounds great."

"It's a date, then. Let me give you my number. You can call me, and then I'll have you in my contacts."

We exchanged numbers, and while we did, I couldn't help but wonder if I was complicating my life further by going out with Sinclair. It *was* just for the ball. Which Cooper and Greyson couldn't go to.

Which, let's be honest, Cooper got a full pass for what was going on with his mom. I was genuinely worried about her and hurting for Cooper. He was as close to his parents as I was to mine. But Greyson? Greyson could have told Lucian no. He'd had the date with me before this trip came up.

None of that stopped me from feeling oddly guilty about how much I was looking forward to this date with Sinclair. On the surface at least, he was pretty much the perfect guy for me. I had to get over the guilt. Going to the ball alone would be a little awkward. And it wasn't like I'd ditched Greyson and Cooper in favor of Sinclair.

He was just the right man at the right time. So, so right.

And I knew Greyson and Cooper couldn't expect me to go solo. With Lark there? They had to know that wasn't going to work for me. They also had to know that if the situation was reversed, I wouldn't expect them not to ask someone else. And also, I hadn't done the asking. Sinclair had.

Who was I to tell the maker of such fine doughnuts no?

I shared the doughnuts with Juniper and Kip, then saved the rest for movie night with Buttercup and Juniper that evening. As we ate our pizza (the doughnuts were for dessert) and got ready to watch our flick, I also shared about my new date for the ball. I told them all about Sinclair and, long story short, they were completely on board with him taking me.

Of course, Juniper had been the one to send him back to my office in the first place, so she was really wound up about him.

His magic with doughnuts didn't hurt, but Buttercup, Goth girl that she was, loved that he was a necromancer. That might have actually been the first time I'd seen a flash of longing in her eyes when talking about my love life.

Like I'd said, Juniper was even more thrilled about it than Buttercup, who'd never been quite as invested in my personal life. Juniper still hadn't totally warmed up to Greyson, and while she liked Cooper and was very sympathetic about his situation with his mom, she agreed that I shouldn't go to the ball solo. She and Pete were going to the ball, too, so it would be nice to have her there with Lark around. Emotional support and all that.

I'd sort of expected them to give me grief about adding a third man to my dating repertoire, but they were all for it. Really, the whole conversation went easier than anticipated.

Easier than trying to decide what to wear on this getting-to-know-you date with Sinclair. I'd been standing in my closet for at least ten minutes, and there were already a few discarded outfits on my bed.

My phone buzzed, giving me a reprieve. I checked the screen. It was Cooper answering my earlier text asking about his mom.

Nothing new. She still refuses to go to the doctor.

That wasn't good. I tried to look on the bright side. *Maybe it's a sign she feels better?*

Maybe. Let's hope.

I am.

Me too.

I put the phone down and went back to standing in my closet.

"Spider," I called out. "What should I wear to

dinner?" I wasn't even sure where he was at the moment.

Apparently, I'd said the magic word since he came scampering in and slid to a stop. "Dinner? Spider loves Chicken Party."

I snorted a laugh. "Do you? I had no idea. Might as well feed you now, huh?"

He meowed a happy little response and trotted off. I followed him into the kitchen, filled his bowl, then went back to my closet while he stuffed his cute, bewhiskered face.

I didn't want anything too fancy or too sexy. This was just a friendly, casual thing. We were not going to be dating beyond the ball. At least, that was my assumption. I mean, let's get real. Despite Juniper and Buttercup's enthusiasm, two guys were enough. Right? Or…I didn't know. Maybe I was overthinking it. This was just a new friend helping me out. A new, super-hot friend.

Regardless, I didn't want to be underdressed or look like a frump for this evening. The guy was taking me out. I wanted to be respectful of his time and efforts.

I settled on a wine-colored long-sleeve wrap dress with a brown leather belt and my brown boots. The dress showed a smidge of cleavage, so it was borderline sexy, but otherwise covered up. This time of year in Nocturne Falls was great because it was cool enough to wear some of my winter things. I added some jewelry and my leather jacket, then grabbed my purse and headed out. After kissing Spider goodbye, of course.

That kiss (and the very important extra belly rubs that followed) made me a little late to meet Sinclair by the warehouse door. Apparently, I had a real knack for attracting the punctual, because he was already there. He'd parked across the street and was leaning against his car, a sleek, all-black SUV that looked a little like a hearse. Or maybe I was projecting.

He was a necromancer, not an undertaker.

He smiled when I came through the door and stopped leaning to stand up straight. "Evening."

"Hi, sorry I'm late." For some reason, I'd expected him in a suit, but he looked like a slightly dressed-up version of the man who'd come to my office. Tight, low-slung dark-wash jeans, a black crew-neck sweater that highlighted just how in shape he was, and a black leather motocross jacket. As I walked toward him, the silver streaks in his hair and the strand of dark beads at his throat gleamed under the streetlight, giving him a kind of supernatural glow.

I didn't want to sound overly dramatic, but with that silvery glow and the black-on-black clothing, he looked like death personified. If death had a modern kind of hipster vibe going on, and was, oh, you know, super sexy.

And this was from a woman who'd actually met death in the form of Greyson's other boss, retired grim reaper Lucian Dupree.

Sinclair laughed as he walked halfway into the street to meet me. "You're right on time. I just got here. You look great, by the way."

"Thanks." I suddenly realized I'd been holding my breath. "You look pretty good yourself." We walked to the car together, then he opened the passenger door for me. I climbed in, put my seat belt on, and waited for him to join me. The car smelled amazing, and my mouth started to water.

He got in and glanced at me. "Why are you smiling like you've just been told a secret?"

"Your car smells like doughnuts."

He snorted as he buckled in. "I do deliveries with this car sometimes. Enough that the smell has kind of stuck, I guess. I don't even notice it anymore." He started the car. "Is it bothering you?"

"Bothering me? If you could bottle that scent and sell it, you'd be a millionaire. It's the best smell ever. Well, it's up there. Top five absolutely."

"I'll put doughnut perfume on my to-do list." He laughed as he pulled away from the curb.

Ten minutes later, we were walking into the Poisoned Apple. The pub wasn't a spot I frequented that often, but I loved the look of the place. All that rich wood paneling and high-sided booths. There was something cozy and mysterious about it. Like a place spies would meet to exchange information. And to me, that just made it seem even more like the perfect upscale British pub. Not that I'd ever been to a real British pub, but in my mind, these walls were the exact shade of dark green you'd find in any classy London tavern.

We went up to the hostess stand and were greeted right away.

"Evening." Sinclair gave his name. "Crowe, party of two for seven fifteen."

The woman checked the book in front of her, then picked up two menus and smiled at us. "Right this way."

We got seated in one of those cozy private booths, the server came by to take our drink orders (a glass of moscato for me, a beer for Sinclair), then we perused our menus.

"Have you eaten here before?" Sinclair asked.

"Yes, but it's been a while. Have you?"

"No, but it was recommended to me by a few people." He looked past the menu at me. "You don't only eat sweets, do you?"

I laughed. "No, I eat regular food too."

"Just checking."

That got me thinking that maybe I should order something healthy. Not to impress him, because I wasn't about to eat a salad just so a guy would think I was, I don't know, ladylike or whatever, but because I probably should eat something that had actual vitamins in it.

Or at least that's how I felt until I saw the house risotto on the menu. I made a little noise of pleasure before I even realized it.

Sinclair set his menu aside. "What was that about?"

"The risotto. Did you see it? Parmesan and shrimp and pancetta with peas and shallots." I put my menu down. "I don't need to look at anything else." Except him, because wow, the man was smoking.

He nodded as he picked his menu up again. "That does sound good, but the hanger steak with duck fat fries is calling my name." He set his menu aside as well. "Should we save room for dessert, or is that a dumb question?"

"There are no dumb questions when it comes to dessert. Also, if you have a thing about people taking food off your plate, I'll warn you now that I will be stealing some of your fries."

He laughed. "Good to know."

Our server came back and we ordered, then we settled back into the purpose of the date. Getting to know each other.

He spoke before I could, which was fine. I was only going to talk about doughnuts anyway. "So, have you heard the big news about the ball?"

"You mean that Elenora hired a DJ instead of her usual live musicians?"

"No, but that is interesting."

"If that's not it, what's the big news, then?"

He leaned in. "Elenora is using the ball to debut a new purchase. One of the rarest diamonds to exist, a flawless pink diamond called the Heart of Dawn. Willa Iscove, the jeweler here in town, just put the finishing touches on the necklace it's in."

"Wow, that is really cool."

"It's something like seventy-five carats and priceless, apparently."

Like most winter elves, my fondness for ice extended beyond the kind made of water. "I can't wait to see it." I also made a mental note to borrow a few extra of the royal family jewels for this bash. I hardly ever wore them, but if there was ever a time to pile them on, the Black and Orange Ball was it. "I guess that explains this year's theme of ice."

"Makes sense now, doesn't it?"

"Totally." I thought about this new information. "How do you know about this diamond? Did Willa tell you?" I hadn't heard a peep, not that I was part of the Ellingham inner circle or anything like that, but Birdie generally knew everything, and she hadn't said a word. Very unlike her.

"It's pretty hush-hush, but I know people who know people. And no, it wasn't Willa. Although I do know her." He sipped his beer.

I gave him my serious stare. "Like who, then?"

He snorted. "Let's just say a little birdie told me."

"I knew it. I just saw her, and she didn't say a word to me." I sat back. "I feel like my social status has just taken a hit. And you're new in town. How did you get to be that deep in her good graces?"

He held his hands out like it was the simplest thing in the world to understand. "I have doughnuts."

"A seventy-five-carat pink diamond, Mom." I stared earnestly into the snow globe. If there was ever a way to persuade my mother to come to the ball, this was it.

"Oh my, that does sound amazing. I would love to see that in person." Her mouth bunched to one side, a sure sign she was thinking hard. "I wonder if your father could spare me for a few days."

"Of course he can. Tell him it's an ice emergency!" I laughed.

She chuckled. "I don't think he'd consider anything diamond-related an emergency. And I already sent the RSVP back with our regrets. You know how hectic this time of year is for us here."

"I know, but I promise Elenora wouldn't be bothered if you changed your mind about coming. She'd probably love it. You're royalty, after all! And it's only a few days. A day down, the day of the ball, then back home the next day."

"True. Although just thinking about all that travel in such a short amount of time is exhausting."

She was right about that. The trip took almost fourteen hours if traveling by standard human means. But she didn't need to do that. I shrugged. "Take the sleigh. Uncle Kris will lend it to you."

"This time of year?" She snorted. "Not likely. You know he likes to run random packing drills and maintenance checks."

"What if Aunt Martha just dropped you off?" I hesitated as a new idea came to me. "Although, if you persuaded her to come to the ball with you, there's no way Uncle Kris would tell you both no. You could fly down that morning and go home that night. Twelve hours tops. He could spare the sleigh for that long."

"Hmm. Maybe." She cocked her head. "You really think you could wrangle a ticket to the ball for her too?"

"I can totally do that." At least I thought I could. Unless Elenora had a cap on the attendance, I couldn't see how she wouldn't want the wives of Jack Frost *and* Santa Claus at her event. North Pole royalty and all that. "You talk to Aunt Martha, see what she thinks, and I'll get in touch with Elenora and confirm that second ticket. And that your invite still stands. Then we'll talk again tomorrow and iron out the details."

"You seem awfully sure this is going to happen. Your uncle could still say no."

"Tell him I'm homesick."

My mother sucked in a breath. "Oh, honey, you are? I will absolutely come. Don't you worry. I'll be there as soon as—"

"Mom."

"I can, and I will definitely bring Aunt Martha with me. You just—"

"Mom."

"Hang on, honey, we're coming. You poor—"

"*Mom*."

She finally took a breath. "What, honey?"

"I'm not homesick. I love it here. Which is not to say I don't miss you guys, I do. But I'm completely settled in here. I just thought if you told Uncle Kris that I was homesick, it would help tip the scales in the right direction."

"Oh! Good thinking. That will definitely help." She smiled at me. "I'm glad you're not really homesick."

"Thanks. And thank you for the care package. I love it! Tell Aunt Martha how much I appreciate it, too, okay?"

"I will. I'll talk to you tomorrow, Jay."

"Bye, Mom." I hit the button to end the call, and the snow in the globe settled as the magical line went dead.

I clutched the globe to my chest and stared up at

the ceiling. It was late and I needed to go to bed, but I couldn't stop thinking about dinner with Sinclair. It had been so good. We'd really clicked. And I'd learned more about him. Who knew that he got a new silver streak in his hair every time he used his magic?

With a sigh, I put the snow globe on the side table and wandered over to the kitchen for one of my mom's orange snickerdoodles. They'd been too good to leave in my office.

I thought about the date some more as I ate the cookie. It had been a great night. He was so easy to talk to, and we had a lot in common. Surprising, considering the kind of supernatural he was, but it was the truth. We both loved sweets, which was good for him seeing as how he had a doughnut shop and all. We also liked funny movies, pizza, books (A man who read! Be still my heart!), and shopping. In fact, he'd asked if I'd like to hit the antique stores with him sometime in search of a lamp for his living room.

But best of all, he had a cat. And get this—she was a sweet little all-white thing named Sugar. Because that was the most perfect name for a white cat owned by a guy who made doughnuts ever. We'd shared photos of our fur babies and stories about them and had even talked about getting them together for a playdate. And speaking of dates, we'd already decided to hit the pet store on our next adventure. Which meant we were going out again.

Couldn't say I was sorry. I liked Sinclair. He was a good guy. So why not go out again? I could date three guys if I wanted to.

Of course, when we were talking about our cats, I did *not* mention Spider's verbal abilities. He spoke only around me anyway, so what was the point? I realized that most of the supernaturals in Nocturne Falls were pretty easygoing about things that would be considered downright freaky in other towns, but a talking cat was still pretty out there. I mean, vampires and werewolves and witches were all real things. Talking cats? Not so much. Not until my Spider.

And sure, I'd just had dinner with a guy who could communicate with the dead, but he was a necromancer. And I was a winter elf. Not Dr. Dolittle.

So Spider's unique gift stayed a secret for now. I ate the last of the cookie as the feline himself sauntered into the room.

He sat by my feet and yawned. "Bedtime, Mama. Spider sleepy."

"Poor baby. Am I keeping you up?" I scooped him into my arms and held him like an infant. He put one paw on my face. I kissed it. "Would you like a girlfriend named Sugar? I bet she would think you're the most handsome kitty she's ever seen."

"What's girlfriend?"

"You know. A friend who's a girl. And a cat. Like Mama has Cooper and Greyson who are boys who are friends."

He blinked up at me as I carried him to the bedroom. "Vampire girl?"

"Nope, just a cat. A lady cat. She's very pretty. I've seen pictures."

"Spider have to share bowl?"

I snort-laughed. "No, she has her own bowl. You don't have to share." I put him on the bed.

He stretched, then flopped down. "Okay girlfriend. Maybe. No sharing."

I shook my head, still smiling. "Oh, Spider, never change." I went into the bathroom to brush the cookie crumbs out of my teeth.

Tomorrow was going to be a very interesting day. I'd never gone to see Elenora Ellingham about anything before, but the prospect of that encounter sent a little nervous trill through me. It was like requesting an audience with the queen. Of dragons.

Elenora was, in my mind anyway, the ultimate power in Nocturne Falls. And while I was true royalty, I had no real sway in this town.

I couldn't help but wonder if Elenora would require something from me in order to grant access to the ball to my aunt and mother. Sort of an exchange of favors, as it were. If she did, that was fine. Up to a certain point. I didn't want to agree to anything blindly.

I sat in Elenora's study the next day wearing a sleek charcoal gray dress, my good pearls, my diamond studs, and a delicate sapphire and diamond bracelet my aunt and uncle had given me as a graduation present. I had dressed to impress, especially after she'd been so quick to invite me over.

Granted, I didn't have a car, so I'd had to call a Ryde to get here, but that's what the corporate account was for.

Elenora smiled at me. "Your pearls are lovely, dear. A family heirloom, am I right?"

I trailed my fingers over them. "Yes, you are. They were a wedding present to my grandmother Frost. My mother had them restrung for me when I turned sixteen." I'd thought they were a nice but boring gift then. Now, I appreciated the necklace and how it had been worn by some of the other women in my family.

She smiled and nodded, looking pleased with herself. "I knew it. There is something uniquely special to the gleam of old, quality pearls. But then, I'd expect the Winter Princess to have nothing less."

"You have a very good eye." I smiled and sipped the tea I'd been offered. It was all so ladylike.

"I like to think so. Jewelry, good jewelry, is

something of a hobby of mine." Her smile grew a little more self-indulgent, and her diamond and ruby ring flashed as she waved her hand. "I have recently acquired a spectacular new piece I'll be debuting at the ball, but then, I suppose you've already heard about it. I know how word travels in this town."

I laughed softly. "I have heard about it, but I'm sure seeing it in person at the ball won't do the rumors justice."

She tipped her head. "Would you like to see it now?"

My mouth came open a little. I hadn't been expecting that. "Yes."

She raised her head to look past me at her assistant, Alice Bishop. The woman was tucked away in the corner of the room reading a book. By which I mean listening in on our conversation. "Alice, would you bring the Heart of Dawn in so Jayne can have a look at it?"

Alice didn't answer, just put her book down and shuffled out of the room.

The diamond couldn't have been far away, because Alice came back thirty seconds later with a large hinged white velvet box. She handed the box to Elenora, then went back to eavesdropping—I mean, reading her book.

"I'm sure you heard I had Willa Iscove set the stone into a necklace."

"I did." I felt odd telling her that. Like I was confirming how much gossip went on in town. But honesty was always the best policy. Especially when I was there in the hopes of getting my aunt and mother into the ball.

She lifted the box lid, and I lost the ability to breathe.

I'd never seen a diamond that big, that pink, or that brilliant. "Wow." My sparkling commentary aside, I was blown away by the contents of the box.

"Jayne Frost, meet the Heart of Dawn. Seven hundred and sixty-five points of flawless pink diamond."

I glanced up at her. "So it's more than seventy-five carats? Amazing. Chillacious is actually the word that comes to mind."

She nodded with approval. "Sounds fitting for a piece of ice like this. And you know your carat weights. Yes, it's a little over. But what's fifteen points here or there?"

The necklace that held the Heart of Dawn was also done in diamonds, all brilliant white and in a variety of shapes that made it look like a cascade of gems held the main stone. "I've never seen anything like it."

Elenora made a small noise of disbelief. "Surely your family has some impressive crown jewels."

"We do, but this is...just amazing." I couldn't stop staring. I forced myself to make eye contact again. "Thank you for the sneak peek. I can only imagine the crowd you're going to have around you at the ball with people trying to get a better look at that gorgeous rock."

She closed the lid gently. "I've hired some extra security, but this is Nocturne Falls, and my private event. Despite the crowd that will attend, I'm not worried."

"No, of course not." I hesitated, then found my courage. "Speaking of the event, that's why I came to see you today. I was really hoping you might be willing to extend that invitation to my mother again. With a plus one for my aunt."

Elenora folded her hands on top of the box. "It would be my pleasure to invite them. Please, tell them it's my honor to host them at the ball. I will consider them my special guests." She lifted a hand to her throat. "It's been centuries since I entertained royalty. I hope I remember the protocol."

"I promise my mom and aunt won't expect any special treatment. They'll just be excited to attend. And between us, I think they'll be a little excited to get out of the Christmas madness that's going on in the North Pole too. Halloween isn't a big deal up there, so this will be a real treat for them."

Elenora smiled. "Well, I look forward to meeting them. Have you told them about the theme?"

"I have. And since we're being up front here, the news about the Heart of Dawn was a big draw for my mom. She and my aunt love jewelry. I'm sure they'll be digging into the royal vaults for some special pieces for the ball."

Elenora's eyes lit up with that particular vampire glow. "Oh, that is wonderful news. The more the merrier."

"Excellent." I stood, not wanting to wear out my welcome. "Thank you so much. I don't want to take up any more of your time than I already have, and I have to get back to the shop anyway. I really appreciate you inviting them."

She stood, keeping a firm grip on the box. "Of course. I'll walk you out."

She didn't speak again until we were in the hall and almost at the door. "I meant to tell you that I appreciate your honesty when you spoke to my grandson. Your attitude is to be commended."

"I don't think I follow." I really didn't.

"About Lark. The young woman I hired to entertain at the ball." She opened the front door for me. "I wouldn't have hired her if you hadn't given the consent. And considering what happened between you, I would have understood if you hadn't."

"Oh. Well…" I shrugged, a little at a loss for words. "It seemed like the right thing to do."

Her smile was thinner this time. "I certainly hope so."

Cooper was walking out of the warehouse as the Ryde dropped me off. There were lines around his eyes, and his eyes held a darkness I wasn't used to.

I hopped out of the car. "What's wrong?" But I had a feeling I already knew.

"My mom was admitted to the hospital this morning with a full-blown case of heatstroke."

"Oh no." My heart ached for him. "Are you leaving to see her, then?"

He swallowed and nodded. "That's why I came by. I'm headed to my parents' today. I'm glad I caught you. You look extra nice. Something going on?"

I was surprised he'd noticed my outfit, considering everything on his mind. "Just a meeting. Nothing big. Are you going straight to the airport?"

"Just have to run by the station first. Not sure when I'll be back, but I wanted to say goodbye."

The sadness in his voice almost killed me. "I'm glad you did." I leaned up and kissed his cheek, then cupped his face in my hands. "She's going to be okay, Coop."

He sighed, the pain in his sky-blue eyes darkening the color to a stormy sea. "I hope you're right."

I dropped my hands, wishing there was more I could do or say to help. "Keep me posted, okay? You and your whole family are in my thoughts. If there's anything I can do, just say the word."

"Thanks. I will." He lifted his head. "Birdie mentioned your mom and aunt are coming into town?"

Thanks to Elenora's generosity. "For the ball."

"Good. I'm glad you're not going alone. I'm sorry about not being there for you."

"Your mom is all that matters. Don't even think about it."

He nodded. "Still, I'm glad you won't be by yourself. Especially since I heard Greyson has to go out of town too."

I thought about Sinclair and how I was going to have to mention him at some point. Now, however, didn't seem like the time. I shrugged. "Things happen."

"That's for sure." Cooper checked his watch. "I better go. I have to grab my stuff from the station before my flight."

"Travel safe."

"Thanks."

We kissed goodbye, then I watched him walk away for a few seconds before I went inside. I had the strangest feeling. Like we were saying goodbye in a much bigger way. I shook my head as I opened my office door. I didn't like the way I was feeling.

I probably needed sugar.

Fortunately, half of the goodies my mom and aunt had sent me were still in my desk drawer. I dug into some of my aunt's eggnog fudge. That wasn't one of the recipes they'd experimented with (you can't improve on perfection), and as I downed that delicious, creamy bite, I started to feel better.

Cooper would be back. His mom would get better. She had to. Then he'd come home.

Work took over for the next few hours, so much so that I toiled away right through lunch and didn't realize it until Juniper stuck her head into my office.

"Hey, did you eat?"

"No." I glanced at the clock on the wall. "Wow, it's almost two." I laughed. "I guess that fudge I ate really filled me up."

She narrowed her eyes. "You have fudge?"

"Yes."

"Eggnog?"

Instead of answering, I just took the container out and held it up. "Help yourself."

She came in and did just that, taking a big piece. "I'll forgive you for holding out, seeing as how you're busy being infatuated with Sinclair."

"I'm not infatuated with him."

"Hah," she managed around a mouthful of fudge.

"I don't know what I am with him. I like him. A lot. We had a great dinner, but he's just a date for the ball. That's it. I mean, one dinner does not a relationship make."

Juni leaned against the filing cabinet. "True. Plus, you still need to figure out Cooper and Greyson."

I sighed. "Speaking of Cooper, he left to go see his mom today."

She nodded. "I know, he stopped in the shop to see if that's where you were after you weren't in your office. He said he was going to call you, but then I saw you two talking outside when I was getting more shopping bags out of the warehouse, so I figured you'd talked."

"We did. He just wanted to say goodbye before he left."

"And Greyson?" She licked the remaining fudge off her fingers.

"He'll be back the night of Halloween. If all goes well."

"Good luck with that. International flights aren't always reliable."

"I know. And I have no idea what this job is for Lucian. But no point in worrying about what I can't change, right?" I stood. "I guess I should eat. I'll just run upstairs and make myself a quick bite."

"Sounds like a plan. But I actually did come in here to tell you something. A little news."

"Oh?"

"Kip's dating some chick who works at Insomnia, and you're never going to believe this, but Lark was a guest DJ there last night. And apparently, she's working three more nights before the ball. They're making a big thing about it, like she's some kind of celebrity."

"She is, sort of. From what I hear, she's really popular in Europe on the club circuit."

Juni snorted. "Whatever. Why does she have to work at Insomnia, though?"

"Well…" I took a breath. "It's not that surprising. I mean, she is a DJ, and Insomnia is a nightclub. And she probably saw the opportunity to make some more money while she was here, so why not?"

Juniper gave me a curious look. "You're not mad?"

"No. Not mad. Not thrilled that she's invaded my new hometown like a virus, but I decided I was going to put the past behind me and move on, so I need to let it go."

Juniper nodded. "Maybe you should call

Sinclair. See if he wants to go clubbing with you. You know, make an appearance."

"No. I don't want her to think I'm checking up on her or anything like that."

"Suit yourself. Personally, I'd want her to know that I was wise to her."

I laughed. "There's nothing to be wise to." I grabbed my purse. "Now I'm going to eat."

And I did, too. A PB & J & F. Which was peanut butter, jelly (strawberry this time), and marshmallow fluff. On wheat bread, because I'm not completely unhealthy. But as I ate, and the sugar refueled me, I thought about what Juniper had said.

Should I casually swing by Insomnia? Or should I ignore the fact that Lark was working there? I wasn't sure. But it did feel like I should at least be keeping up with her to some extent. Especially after what Elenora had said about hoping I'd made the right decision. What could that have possibly meant? There was no way that being okay with Lark getting that job could have some kind of impact on my life, positive or negative.

Ugh. Life had suddenly gotten so complicated. But I kind of had a secret weapon. An inside source, as it were.

I tapped my phone's screen, brought up my contacts, and scrolled through them, then dialed the one person I could always rely on to keep me up to date on what was happening in town.

Hopefully, she could tell me if she'd heard anything from Elenora.

She answered on the second ring. "Princess! How are you?"

"Just fine, Birdie. How are you?"

"Peachy. Which is mostly because I had cobbler for lunch. Boy, do I love that stuff. What's happening?"

"Nothing much. Just wanted to see if you were up for breakfast tomorrow morning? We haven't been out to breakfast in a while."

"No, we haven't, and yes, I am. Mummy's?"

"Is there anywhere else?"

She laughed. "I'll see you there at eight. Sound good?"

"Sounds perfect."

The next morning, I was so jazzed to see Birdie and catch up that I got to Mummy's early. Don't act so shocked, it happens. I grabbed a couple menus, found a booth, and settled in to wait. I read the menu to occupy myself, which was actually highly enjoyable given that it combined my love of reading with my love of food. There was a little card clipped to the top of the inside page, announcing the day's specials. I skimmed it, then read it again more thoroughly to make sure my eyes hadn't deceived me.

Chocolate chunk and potato chip pancakes? That was so weird, and yet, there was something pretty intriguing about the potential of that sweet, salty combination.

"Hello, dollface. What can I get you?"

I looked up to see Arty smiling down at me. "Hey, hi. I thought you only worked the counter."

"Nope. I go where I'm needed. How are you this morning?"

"Great, how are you?" His pompadour was in full pomp.

"I'm fine and dandy and sweet as candy. You here by your lonesome?"

"No, Birdie Caruthers is joining me."

"Well, now, the Winter Princess and the unofficial mayor of Nocturne Falls? Today is my lucky day. What can I get you while you wait?"

"Coffee."

"You got it. Sure you don't want a cinnamon bun to go with it?"

"No, I'm saving myself for those potato chip pancakes."

He nodded. "Smartest thing you'll do all day. Trust me."

"That good, huh?"

"They'll make you stupid with happiness." He winked. "Be right back with your cuppa. And I'll bring one for Ms. Birdie, too."

"Thank you." As soon as he walked away, I saw Birdie by the door. I waved her over. "Hey, good morning."

She didn't look like her usual happy self. "Morning. I don't know about good."

"What's going on?"

She leaned in and lowered her voice. "There were three robberies last night. *Three.*" She shook her head. "That just doesn't happen in this town."

No, it didn't. At least not that I'd ever heard about. "What the heck is going on? Do you know who did it?"

Arty came back with two coffees. "I'll give Your Highnesses a moment to settle in." Then he slipped away like he knew we were in the middle of something.

Birdie upended the sugar dispenser into her coffee as she stirred. "No leads on who did it. Not even a best guess. All three thefts were against tourists. And…" She leaned in again. "They were all supernaturals."

My eyes widened. "Okay, that's just bold. Somebody's got snowballs the size of planets to make supers their target."

Birdie nodded. "Right? It's very frustrating. Hank's in a terrible mood, as you can imagine."

Her nephew, the sheriff, wasn't exactly known for his bubbly personality to begin with. "Yikes. I don't envy you being in that office today."

She waved the words away as she sipped her now heavily sweetened and lightened java. "Oh, he wouldn't dare fuss at me. Not after I pulled the

CCTV footage from one of the B&Bs that got hit."

"Well, that should help." I added sugar and cream to my own cup.

"You'd think so, but all the cameras caught was a blur going by. Pretty sure it was a moth." She sighed. "And unless we have a moth shifter in town, that's not going to help."

I made a face. "Is that a thing? Because I've never heard of that."

Before she could answer, Arty was back. "You ladies ready to order?"

Birdie picked up her menu. "Go ahead, Princess. I'll figure out my order while you place yours."

"Okay." I glanced at him. "I want that pancake special with a side of bacon."

"You got it. Maple syrup or the peanut butter sauce?"

Peanut butter sauce? How had I missed that? "Which one do you recommend?"

"Both," he said. "You could be hit by a bus on your way to work. Live while you can."

I grinned and handed him my menu. "Good point."

Birdie turned her menu over as well. "I'll have the meat lover's omelet, cheese grits, and hash browns, extra crispy. Plus a cinnamon bun for here and another boxed to go."

"Coming up!" Arty headed away to put our order in.

Birdie glanced at me. "I can't help it. I'm a stress-eater."

I refrained from commenting about how this morning's order didn't seem any different than her usual order. Instead, I held my hands up. "You don't have to explain to me."

She smiled. "That's one of the things I love about you." She straightened her place mat. "Now, about your date for the ball—"

"I already have one, so you don't have to add that to your list of things to be stressed about."

Her brows shot up. "You do? Who?"

I hesitated. "Sinclair Crowe. He owns—"

"Zombie Donuts."

"You know him?"

She snorted. "Who did you think I was going to set you up with?"

A little part of me sank. "You sent him to my office?"

"Heavens, no. Why? Did he show up there?"

"Yes. With a large box of very delicious doughnuts."

"Hmm. That would have been a good idea, had I thought of it. But I didn't. I confess, I have been so busy at the station, and then I had volunteered to help at Charlie's school with their Christmas play, and my time sort of slipped away from me. I hadn't gotten around to talking to Sin yet. I'm so glad you two met anyway." She batted her eyelashes at me. "Isn't he dreamy? Tell me everything."

Laughing, I shook my head. "There isn't much to tell." But I felt better knowing he'd shown up on his own. There was something about being set up that felt so forced to me. Like I would have struggled to be myself or something.

I gave her the light version of us meeting, agreeing to go to the ball, and our one dinner at the Poisoned Apple, then before she could dig for more details, I brought up the news that my mom and aunt were coming to the ball, too.

She clapped her hands. "That is so exciting. I cannot wait to meet them. What do I call your mother? Your Highness? Your Majesty? Oh, Your Grace?"

I knew *Mrs. Frost* would never satisfy her, so I went with the most informal title I could think of. "Lady Frost. And you can call my aunt Mrs. Kringle. I promise, that's what everyone calls her."

She narrowed her eyes at me. "If you say so."

"I do."

Arty showed up with our food, and my stomach rumbled in appreciation. He put the plates in front of us, wished us bon appétit, and left us to chow down. Which we did. The pancakes were, to use Arty's word, *stupid* good.

When we came up for air, I used the moment to dig into the subject I most needed to know about.

"Hey, do you know how Lark came to be DJing at Insomnia?"

Birdie nodded and swallowed a bite of omelet. "I do. Through Greyson."

"What?" That didn't make me happy at all. He knew how I felt about her.

"Before you get mad at him, it wasn't his fault. The way I hear it, when Lucian sent him off to Rome, Greyson tried to get out of the trip by telling him you needed him at the ball. Then he explained why you needed him, and one thing led to another. Lucian apparently thought having a famous DJ at his club would bring more people in."

I sighed. "Has it?"

"Yes. You know Chet? He's a doorman there?"

"Yep, I know him." I was only mildly acquainted with the bear shifter, but he was always friendly to me when I went to the club.

"Well, his mother is in my bunco group, and she said the first night Lark worked, they had double the usual crowd. Chet had to call in a second bouncer."

"Wow. I didn't know she was *that* popular."

Birdie shrugged. "Who would have thought someone could make a name for themselves playing records by other people?"

"I think there's more to it than that."

"Probably. But still." Birdie loaded her fork with

crispy hash browns. "Seems to me like she's made a career out of other people's talents."

I took another bite of pancakes. I wasn't going to argue. I also wasn't going to Insomnia. Call me petty, but I didn't want to be one more face in the crowd clamoring to see the Ice Queen drop some beats.

October thirty-first arrived with the kind of bright chill that made you want to suck down a couple pumpkin spice lattes and enjoy the brilliance of the changing leaves while wearing your favorite oversize cardigan.

I, however, had work to do.

My aunt and mom were due to arrive after lunch, and by five, we'd be in the throes of Black and Orange Ball preparations. There was hair and makeup to be done, fancy dresses to get into, sparkling jewelry to adorn ourselves with, and snazzy shoes to slip on. It would be a whirlwind of female activity.

I couldn't wait.

But due to the conspicuous nature of the large, magical, cherry-red sleigh they were arriving in, the decision had been made to land said sleigh at Elenora's estate. She had the room and the ability to hide the vehicle from curious eyes in one of her detached garages. She'd also graciously offered to have her driver bring my mom and aunt to the shop.

I thought it was a very nice thing for her to do, but I also figured Elenora was enjoying the prestige of having North Pole royalty arrive at her home and the one and only Santa's sleigh temporarily housed on her property. And I knew my mom and aunt were going to thoroughly enjoy being welcomed to town by Elenora's lavish brand of hospitality.

How did I know that? I'd offered to meet them at Elenora's, and they'd told me not to worry about it and they'd see me at the shop because they didn't want to take me away from my work until it was absolutely necessary. Which was very understanding of them, because I had tons to do, but clearly, the draw of having a four-hundred-year-old vampire and former duchess all to themselves was more than they could resist.

I'm sure they were also hoping for an advance peek at the Heart of Dawn. I had no doubt Elenora would indulge them. I wasn't sure if they'd be opening their jewelry boxes as well, but if they did, Elenora would not be disappointed. My mom and aunt were bringing some of the good stuff from the royal vaults. I was pretty excited to see it myself.

Not as excited as I was to see Sinclair, however.

See him again, I should add. We'd been out quite a few times since he'd first shown up in my office. I was especially interested in his costume this evening as he'd told me he was going as snow at midnight, which was both interesting and vague. I couldn't wait to see what he looked like.

Introducing him to my mom and aunt would also be interesting. I'd been pretty quiet about Cooper and Greyson, but that was all going to have to come out too. Not sure what they were going to think.

Or if they'd approve. I tended to think not. Especially about Cooper. They'd been the ones to nurse my broken heart back into reasonable shape. They knew very well how hurt I'd been.

As for Greyson…there was that whole thing where he was a vampire. My family was pretty open-minded, but I was next in line for the Winter Throne and I wasn't sure how they'd feel about the possibility that a vampire might be the queen's consort. Not, and I repeat, *not* that I was remotely thinking about marriage with anyone. But that's the exact leap the minds of my mother and aunt would take.

I was already bracing myself for the onslaught of questions. My real goal, besides having them like my friends and my life here in Nocturne Falls, was to keep them from sharing too much with my dad and uncle.

Wasn't like they'd make a corporate decision to pull me out of here based on who I was dating, but I was still my father's daughter, and if he didn't like something, he wasn't going to be quiet about it.

Pretty sure he'd make a point to visit in a very official way as soon as Christmas was over. And that would be the adult equivalent of being called into the principal's office. Except in this case, the principal would be coming to me.

I sighed and tapped my pen on my desk. All this thinking wasn't getting any work done. I went back to it, but a few hours later, I put the pen down and headed into the shop to see if there was anything that needed doing that might get my mind off the uncomfortable conversations to come.

Juniper was fixing the display of Pocket Pets, and Kip was helping a customer.

"Hey, how's it going? You guys need me for anything?"

Juniper frowned as she straightened. "I think I have bad news."

"You think? What's going on?"

She put her hands on her hips and stared at the display. "This inventory isn't adding up. I have a feeling someone stole a Pocket Pet."

I groaned. More fun news to share with my family. "That sucks. Did it just happen?"

"No, it happened yesterday. I've been running the numbers and going over the receipts, and I can't get them to come out right. That's the only answer I can come up with."

"Well, it's not your fault. The store gets busier and busier the closer we get to Christmas. It's bound to happen, sadly. But I'd still like to put the thief on ice."

"Me too. I hated to tell you, especially with your mom and aunt about to arrive, but putting it off wasn't going to make it magically disappear."

"You did the right thing."

"I promise we'll be extra vigilant."

"I know you will be. I think you should call it into the sheriff's department, though."

"Really?"

I nodded. "There have been some other thefts in town in the last few weeks. Not sure this is related, but it still needs to be reported."

"Okay, I'll take care of it."

"Thanks."

"When do your mom and aunt get here?"

A sleek black limo pulled up outside. "Pretty sure they just did."

Grinning, I went out to greet them, opening the limo door before the driver could get to it. "Mom! Aunt Martha!"

"Jayne!" they both yelled. They climbed out and hugged me, causing a small traffic jam on the sidewalk. I hugged them back, so happy to see them I could almost cry. No, I wasn't looking forward to telling them about my love life, but that was a minor part of this trip. They were my family and I loved them.

"How are you guys?" I asked as we finally disengaged.

Aunt Martha cupped my face in her hands, apparently not done greeting me. "You're too skinny. Are you working too hard? I bet you're working too hard."

"I'm working just enough, I promise. And I eat plenty, which is why I am definitely not skinny. You do not have to worry about that."

My mother smiled, making her eyes twinkle. "It's so good to see you, honey."

"You, too. Both of you. Come on in and see the shop."

"What about the luggage?" Aunt Martha asked.

The driver had just come around from the trunk with several large bags that he added to the steamer trunk already sitting on the sidewalk.

"Um, I thought you were only coming for the ball. Did you change your mind? Are you staying over?"

Aunt Martha laughed. "No, silly, this is just for tonight."

"Wow. You two really need some lessons in packing light."

My mother shrugged. "There is no such thing as packing light when you're bringing gowns."

"You should have sent all that through the Santa's Bag."

My mother gave me a look that said I wasn't grasping the gravity of the situation. "That's fine for toys and reports and care packages, but these are custom-made gowns and the royal jewels. Not to mention the shoes your aunt and I had made in Paris. I'm not letting any of that out of my sight."

I just smiled and nodded. "I completely understand. Good thing the building has an elevator."

By six thirty, we were all finally in my apartment and almost ready. I say almost because there seemed to be an endless number of small things that needed doing. Makeup touched up. Shoes buckled tighter. Then looser. Then back to where they started. Tiaras to be adjusted, diamonds to be given one last polish, rings to be added, then subtracted, then, you guessed it, added again.

Of course, it had taken us longer than I'd anticipated to get started because my mom and aunt had spent more time in the store than I'd thought they would. They loved Juniper and probably would have spent all night talking to her if I hadn't reminded them that she was going to be at the ball as well.

I also got the sense that my mom and aunt were very conscious of the fact that they were representing the Winter Court, as it were. Sure, I was the Winter Princess, but they outranked me. There was no question that they were going to be scrutinized this evening.

They really had nothing to worry about, though.

My mother's ensemble was a gorgeous, iridescent deep blue gown. The fabric was a fae weave, designed to capture the brilliance and movement of the northern lights. And it did. With every step she took, a multitude of colors danced across her skirts. I'd worn a dress of the same fae fabric in black to the party Elenora had thrown in honor of the Sandman's visit, but this deep blue was breathtaking.

Mom paired the gown with the Frost tiara, earrings, and necklace, a breath-taking collection of hundreds of carats of diamonds set off by fiery blue opals, the largest of which sat at the center of the necklace and was easily the size of my thumb. She also wore a diamond bracelet that was about an inch wide. A simple silver filigree mask completed the outfit.

She looked every inch the queen she was.

My aunt, on the other hand, had decided to go full-on Mrs. Santa Claus. She knew it was what people would expect, and she wasn't one to disappoint, especially not at a costume ball. Her red velvet dress was trimmed in white sequins and adorned with a large black patent-leather belt, complete with a bejeweled black rhinestone buckle.

To further gild the lily, she'd added her favorite ruby and diamond hair clips, necklace, and bracelet.

The look was perfect on her. A very over-the-top version of her, but just what the ball called for. Together, my mom and aunt looked exactly like what they were: the best part of the Winter Court. Beautiful, regal, magical, and lovely.

Pride overwhelmed me that these amazing women were my family.

But I've kind of glossed over what else was in that steamer trunk. My mom and aunt had brought me a gown. I'd been planning on wearing my beautiful ice-blue coronation gown. They, however, had other plans. Secret plans.

They'd had a new dress made for me. And it was spectacular.

Pure white silk covered in a snowflake pattern of beads, pearls, and crystals, the off-the-shoulder gown could have easily gone in a very bridal direction, if not for the body-hugging shape and the strands of additional beads draped down the back and off each shoulder. Those made it more femme fatale than blushing bride.

With the addition of my personal snowflake tiara, the matching snowflake earrings, and a wide diamond bracelet borrowed from my mother's collection, I was the embodiment of snow.

I added the white bejeweled mask they'd brought me and stood in front of the mirror. I was a little breathless at their gift as my mother clasped the final piece of jewelry, the snowflake necklace, around my neck. The centerpiece diamond was a rare, pale blue cushion-cut stone about the size of a dime. I'd never worn the full snowflake set before. "You guys…I had no idea you were doing this. It's amazing."

Aunt Martha clasped her hands in front of her chest. "You look like a winter dream, Jaynie."

My mother stepped back, smiling and maybe a little bit teary. "You look beautiful. And you deserve it. You've been working so hard, and we're so proud of you."

"I—"

A knock at the door interrupted me. I stiffened, realizing it had to be Sinclair. Introductions would be next. I smiled nervously, and all my previous concerns came walloping up over me. I took a breath and headed for the door. "I'll get that."

"Ooo, that must be your escort for the evening," my aunt cooed.

"Yes." What else could I say? After everything they'd done for me, after how they'd proclaimed their love and pride for me, I just hoped they didn't freak out about the man on the other side of the door.

Wasn't every day you introduced your mom and aunt to a necromancer, after all.

Sinclair's costume of snow at midnight made perfect sense now that I saw him in it. Essentially, his suit was a tux that had been designed to go from standard black at the shoulders to pure white from about his waist on down. That color change wasn't a gradual blend, however, it was done with a pattern of falling snowflakes, and each one had been decorated in small, iridescent crystal. The bottoms of his trouser legs were completely bedazzled as if the snow had piled up there and frozen over. He even had on matching bedazzled shoes. Which I was secretly coveting. His mask was simple black satin and added a hint of roguishness.

The outfit was impressive, not just for its cleverness but because he was bold enough to wear it. I couldn't imagine Cooper or Greyson in anything so...glittery. But his suit could not have complemented my gown better if he'd tried.

His eyes widened and he took a step back. "You look…wow, I don't have the vocabulary to do you justice. You look beautiful and ethereal and way too good to be going out with a guy like me."

I laughed softly and blushed a little. "You look perfect. And very handsome." And he did. The black and white of his tux was perfectly suited to his silver-streaked hair. And there was something undeniably sexy about a guy who could wear a costume with that much sparkle on it and still look like he could kill you with a glance. The man was the most interesting combination of classy and dangerous. Like James Bond, if 007 could wield death magic.

And while I knew I shouldn't be comparing Sinclair to Greyson or Cooper, I was a little. At least to Greyson, because there wasn't as much road to travel between vampire and necromancer as there was between summer elf and necromancer. Plus, Greyson was very much the bad boy. Sinclair, on the other hand, had that going for him too, but in a much more polished, grown-up way. He wasn't so much a bad boy as he was a dangerous man.

My mother cleared her throat, and I jumped, reminded that I was not alone. "Sinclair, won't you come in and meet my mom and my aunt?"

I opened the door to let him in, turning to face them as I did. "Mom, Aunt Martha, this is Sinclair Crowe. My date for the evening. Sinclair, this is my mother, Klara Frost, the Winter Queen, and my aunt, Martha Kringle, the Mother of Christmas."

He bowed. "Lady Frost, Lady Kringle, it's my honor and privilege to meet you both." He straightened, smiling. "It's not difficult to see where Jayne gets her good looks. You ladies are absolutely stunning."

Aunt Martha beamed. Outside of dessert and my uncle Kris, there wasn't much she loved more than a compliment from a charming man, and Sinclair had charm to spare. "That's very kind of you, Mr. Crowe."

"Please, call me Sinclair, if that's not too informal. We're going to be spending the evening together after all."

"Sinclair it is, then," my aunt said. "And you should call us Klara and Martha."

My mother was a bit more reserved. "What is it you do, Sinclair?"

"I own a doughnut shop."

"Mom, remember that box I sent last week?" Sinclair had made up a large box especially for me and shrink-wrapped it so that the doughnuts would stay good and fresh. Then I'd sent it through the Santa's Bag. I considered it hedging my bets, and I was hoping it had worked.

My mom looked at me. "Zombie Donuts?"

"That's the one."

"Horrible name." She smiled. "But fantastic

doughnuts. We enjoyed those very much, and now I know why Jayne sent them. Your shop must do well."

Score one for the princess.

His mouth curved in a humble smile. "It does all right. I'm so glad you enjoyed the doughnuts."

My mother extended her hand. "It's a pleasure to meet you, Sinclair. And very kind of you to accompany my daughter to the ball this evening. Your costume is a perfect match for Jayne's."

He shook her hand. "Thank you." He glanced at me, his gaze filled with pleasure. He'd hit the nail on the head with his choice in tux, and he knew it. "It's almost like we were meant to be."

I smoothed the skirt of my gown as I smiled. Things were going well. "This dress was a complete surprise, too. My mom and aunt Martha had it made for me. But we do look like a pair now, don't we?"

"We do," he answered. "And I'm glad you approve of my tux."

He turned back to my mom and aunt. "If you ladies are ready, there's a limo waiting for us downstairs. There's also another box of doughnuts in there. In case anyone forgot to eat dinner."

Aunt Martha let out a small gasp. "Dinner! We haven't had a bite since lunch."

I laughed. "There will be food at the ball, you know. But probably not doughnuts." I hooked my thumb toward the door. "Let's go."

Spider was sleeping in my closet, and Buttercup had promised to come check on him when she closed the shop, so I decided not to disturb him with a kiss goodbye. Also, black cat hair would not be the best accessory for this gown.

Sinclair offered his arm to my aunt, who took it and immediately started asking what flavors he'd brought. They headed for the elevator while my mom stayed with me as I locked the apartment.

"He seems nice," she said.

"He is. Very nice."

"But? What aren't you telling me? It has something to do with the darkness around him, I'm sure of that."

Snowballs. Why did my mother have to be so perceptive? I made a little half-frown and kept my voice low as I answered. "He's a necromancer."

There was no point in hiding the truth, and I'd much rather she heard it from me than someone at the ball.

Her brows lifted a tiny bit, but more like she was mulling the news over as opposed to being surprised by it. "I've never met one before, but I'm glad I have now."

"You're okay with it?"

"Is there a reason I shouldn't be?"

I almost sighed in relief. "No. There isn't."

"Unless he does something to give me a reason not to like him, I have no issues with you keeping company with Sinclair. And unlike Cooper, who's already got one black mark against him from your college days, and the vampire, who I can't speak about at all, at least Mr. Crowe is actually here for you this evening."

My mouth gaped open. So much for my big secret. "You know about Cooper and Greyson?"

Her smile was a little sly and very knowing. It was a smile I'd seen all my life. "Honey, I'm your mother. And you are heir to the Winter Throne. Do you really think I'm not keeping tabs on you?"

Who in town was providing her with this information? Birdie? I didn't quite believe that. Birdie wouldn't have been able to keep quiet about her connection to my mother. "But you never said anything."

"And tip my hand?" She snorted softly. "Child, please."

"Well, you must also know that they both have very good reasons for their absence this evening."

"I do. But you're my daughter, and you will always be my first concern."

"You two are going to make us late," Aunt Martha called out.

Sinclair was holding the elevator. "Ladies, far be it for me to hurry you along, but…Elenora is waiting."

"Right. Coming." I tucked my keys into my evening bag and hooked my arm through my mother's. "Have you told Dad any of this?"

She laughed as we walked toward the elevator. "Have you seen him here? Because if he knew you were dating the boy who broke your heart in college, he'd have issued a royal decree about that one."

"I'm sure." We stepped onto the elevator, and Sinclair let the doors close. My father wasn't known for his subtly when it came to his opinions on things like that.

Once we were in the limo, the subject thankfully changed from my love life to the ball and the doughnuts Sinclair had brought. He explained what each one was, describing the flavors so we could pick the one we thought we'd like the best. There were three of the Dr Preppers. The man had only known me a short while, but he learned fast.

We managed to make it to the ball without getting a smidge of icing on our fancy clothes, something I considered a personal success. Sinclair walked us to the double doors of Elenora's mansion, and we presented our invitations to one of the two doormen there.

They immediately opened the doors wide and bowed. "Welcome to the Black and Orange Ball."

The four of us strode in like rock stars and were escorted by one of several hosts to the main ballroom. I tried to brace myself for seeing Lark, but the place was fairly crowded and her DJ booth was up on one of the balconies. I could see her, but she wasn't looking my way. She was bent over her equipment, holding the earpiece of some headphones to one ear. A guy with deep blue hair and a matching goatee stood beside her, watching her like he was waiting for a command. That had to be Lance, the boyfriend. Not my cup of tea, but good for her. I could only see them from about the rib cage up because of the equipment.

I stopped looking. I couldn't lie. I was happy that she was a floor away. And even though Cooper had said she liked to walk around in the crowd, I hoped maybe she wouldn't do that here. Who knew? Maybe Elenora had asked her to stay in her booth. Leave the guests alone. That would be just fine with me.

With that small bit of business behind me, I focused on how beautifully decorated the ballroom was. It had been transformed into a cross between a jewelry showroom and a winter wonderland. Long strands of crystals with large, rhinestone snowflakes at the ends hung from the ceiling. Stark-white trees were swathed in more rhinestone ornaments, crystal strands, and loads of fairy lights, making them sparkle.

Enormous arrangements of white and ivory flowers in tall crystal vases were positioned at various spots around the room, some with more swags of snowflakes between them, making a canopy over some of the entrances.

Strategically placed projectors cast moving snowflakes over everything, and the servers were all dressed in white as well, with white masks. Drifts of fake snow throughout added another convincing wintry touch.

The only other nod to Halloween besides the masks on the servers were the pumpkins that seemed to be everywhere, and they were all painted white then covered in fake snow crystals or bedazzled in patterns of rhinestones. I approved. The place was beautiful.

Judging from the ooo's and ahh's, my mom and aunt thought so too. Most of the people around us were also admiring the decorations. I scanned the crowd for familiar faces and saw quite a few, but where was the hostess? Elenora was nowhere to be found. Maybe putting some finishing touches on something.

I glanced up at the DJ booth again, unable to help myself. Lark's boyfriend was at the balcony's edge, staring down at the increasing crowd and bobbing his head to the music. As for that, it wasn't anything like what I'd expected. It had a gentle, sort of techno-tribal beat, and it wasn't so loud that you couldn't talk. I imagined the dancing would come after dinner, and then the party atmosphere would turn up a notch. Right now, the vibe was more cocktail hour than rave. I was good with that. I loved to dance, but my gown wasn't exactly made for getting one's groove on.

Sinclair leaned in. "Really something, huh?"

"Yes. Elenora has outdone herself."

My mother nodded. "The decorations are impeccable."

The crowd had thickened considerably in the few minutes since we'd arrived. The party was in full swing now, and a new team of servers was mixing in with trays of small bites and glasses of champagne.

Aunt Martha was busy flagging down a server with champagne. "Let's have a toast," she said.

We all took a glass, then Aunt Martha raised hers. "To seeing my darling niece again." Then she looked at Sinclair. "And making new friends. And doughnuts."

He grinned as he raised his glass. "Hear, hear."

We all took a sip as the music quickened and the lights dimmed. Lark's voice filled the space. "Ladies and gentlemen, welcome to *the* event of the year in Nocturne Falls, the Black and Orange Ball. Please join me in greeting our generous hostess this evening, who is debuting her very own spectacular piece of ice, the inspiration for tonight's theme, the Heart of Dawn. Here she is now, the gracious Elenora Ellingham."

A spotlight focused on the top of the stairs. Elenora stood in the center of the beam, smiling.

She waved to the crowd as she began to descend. With her regal posture and stiff-armed wave, she would have fit right in at court. Applause went up in great waves, but I had no doubt where all eyes were focused.

Namely, on the enormous pink, heart-shaped diamond around her neck.

Even though I'd seen it before, it was still impossibly beautiful, and in the spotlight it gleamed like a lighthouse beacon. Elenora wore an icy blue structured brocade gown that gave off hints of pink iridescence as she moved. Her mask was of the same fabric. The whole look was the perfect complement to the dazzling jewel at her throat.

At the first landing, she stopped and accepted a glass of champagne from the server waiting there. She lifted it. "Thank you all for joining me this evening. It gives me great pleasure to welcome you into my home for this event. Happy Halloween!"

Cries of "Happy Halloween" echoed back to her, and we all drank. Then the music swelled and she joined the crowd.

I spent the remainder of the time before the dinner chimes sounded introducing my mom and aunt to everyone who came up to say hi. Every so often, I'd glance up at the DJ booth. When Lance wasn't at Lark's side, he was watching the crowd. And once, when Elenora was talking to my mom and aunt, his eyes were on us.

Well, them, really. At least until Lark called him back for something. I felt for him a little. It seemed like Lark had him on a short leash, and from the way he was focused on the crowd, it was pretty clear he'd rather be enjoying the party up close and personal.

But hey, I wasn't about to get broken up over it. He'd made his choices. And I had my family around me and a very sexy, charming man at my side.

I had plenty to keep me busy.

Dinner was delicious, not that Elenora would serve anything that wasn't. Rumor was, the chefs were flown in from Paris, but then, I also heard someone else say that the chefs were fae and the food was laced with magic. I wasn't quite sure about that one, but with Elenora, who knew?

Whoever prepared the food, I was happy the portions were small. That might sound odd coming from me, but my gown wasn't exactly a pair of yoga pants. And I knew dessert was yet to come. Hugh Ellingham had given a toast at dinner and announced that the last and sweetest course, provided by his wife's shop, Delaney's Delectables, would be served later during the dancing.

I was ready for it. Because, you know, sugar. And I loved Delaney's creations so much they'd become a slight addiction. So with the promise of sweets to come, I decided I could manage a little dancing despite my outrageous gown.

Especially when Sinclair held out his hand and said, "Dance with me, sweetness."

How did you say no to that? You didn't.

We danced two songs, then he took a turn with both my mom and aunt, who'd already danced with a few other gentlemen. After a break for the dessert course (so much deliciousness I nearly wept), I danced once with Pete, too, mostly because Juniper made him. And while he was a nice guy (and perfect for Juniper), I was happy to get back to Sinclair.

He was a great dancer, and as the night wore down, I was pleased that Lark's selections got a little slower, allowing for some up close and personal time with Sinclair. I had to give her props—she knew how to keep a room going and how to shift the tone in a way that seemed just right.

I held on to him and let him lead me around the floor. He was so light on his feet that we seemed to float by the other couples. The glasses of champagne I'd had probably contributed to that, but hey, it was a party.

"Having fun?" he asked.

"So much. You?"

He smirked slightly. "More than I thought I would."

I raised my brows. "You didn't think coming to the ball with me would be fun?"

Laughing, he shook his head. "I didn't have any doubts about you. But when you told me your mother and aunt were coming, I thought things might get a bit tense. I don't always go over so well with parents, as you can imagine."

"I don't see why not."

"Jayne, you know what I am." Some of the joy left his gaze. "I'm not exactly who most parents dream of as a partner for their daughter."

I got that. I didn't know what to say exactly, but I didn't want him to be unhappy either. He was a really good guy. And except for most vampires, none of the supernaturals I knew had chosen to be what they were.

Like me, they were born into their kind.

"Sin, listen, who cares about what other people think? You're great. Kind and sweet and a real gentleman. And if anyone can't see that or they judge you just because of your particular brand of gifts, then frost them. They don't deserve your time anyway."

His smile came back. "You think I'm great?"

I laughed. Such a guy. "Yeah, I do."

"Does that mean you'd still like to go out with me even after your *boyfriends* come back to town?"

I smiled and sucked my bottom lip into my mouth while I gave that a nanosecond of thought.

"Yes, I would. If you can handle that."

He shrugged as he spun me around. "Beats not seeing you. And those boys don't intimidate me."

"Boys?" I snickered. "They're grown-ups, I promise. Cooper's my age, and Greyson is a vampire, so he's—"

"They're still boys." He dipped me, his mouth inches from mine. "You deserve more."

He brought me upright again, but held me against him. I was a little breathless. The warmth of his body seemed to penetrate through all the layers of fabric between us as he looked into my eyes, his gaze sparking with mischief. "You deserve me."

"Oh?" That was the best I could do while staring into the master of death's captivating scrutiny and wondering if he was about to kiss me.

He nodded, his mouth so close to mine I could feel his breath on my cheek. "You should be treated like the incredible woman you are. Appreciated. Adored. Swept off your feet." He brushed his lips across my jaw on the way to my ear. "You'll see," he whispered.

The promise, combined with his breath on my ear and the tone of his voice, raised goose bumps on my skin. I shivered, glad we were deep in the crowd and out of sight of my mom and aunt. Not that I was in any way ashamed of Sin. I just wanted this moment to myself.

I regained enough of my senses to answer. "You talk a big game."

"I never make promises I can't keep. I know better than most how short life can be." His eyes gleamed anew with what seemed best described as unbridled happiness. "Like I said...you'll see."

He moved me around him, taking his arm over his head and bringing me to his other side. He was smooth, I'd give him that. "Is this part of being swept off my feet? The dancing?"

"Just scratching the surface." He lifted my arm this time and went under, and I was back where I'd started. "I did bring you a present, though."

"The doughnuts, right?"

He snorted. "Doughnuts aren't so much a present as they are just a truly outstanding perk of dating me."

Okay, I had to admit, Sinclair got better pretty much every time he opened his mouth. "So... what's the present?"

"Follow me."

He swept me off the dance floor and outside to the enormous balcony that overlooked Elenora's elaborate gardens. There were other couples out there, and a few walking in the gardens, all of whom were either hand in hand or arm in arm. I could see why. With the moon shining down and the subtle landscape lighting, the gardens were a very romantic place. Almost magically so. Dark and dim and quiet.

We stopped at the railing. Sinclair dug into his jacket pocket and pulled something out. "For you."

He opened his palm. On it lay a delicate bracelet of dark faceted beads mixed with a few smaller silver ones. Even in the weak light, I could tell that the black beads were giving off a colorful gleam.

"It's gorgeous. I've never seen anything like it. What are those stones?"

"They're rainbow obsidian. Necromancers believe obsidian of any kind is a powerful protector."

I looked up at him. "You wear a strand of these around your neck." I'd caught a glimpse of them a few times before.

"I do."

"They're gorgeous." I held out my wrist. "I love it. Thank you. I want to put it on right now."

He hesitated. "It doesn't really go with your outfit. Or the rest of your jewelry. Especially that diamond bracelet you're already wearing."

"It goes perfectly. Will you put it on me? Right next to the diamonds." It was a beautiful bracelet, but I was more impressed with the kindness and sincerity of the gesture. We hadn't known each other very long, and I certainly hadn't expected anything from him, but the idea that he'd want me protected was very sweet.

He clasped the bracelet around my wrist, and I turned it, watching the stones shimmer with color.

"It really is pretty. Thank you. And to think, I didn't get you a thing."

"Yes, you did."

I looked up at him. "I did?"

He slipped his hands around my waist and drew me in, smiling. "You got me this amazing evening. I wouldn't have come tonight if you hadn't needed a date. In fact, I've gotten out of the house and away from work more in the last week and a half with you than I have since I moved here. Thank you for that."

How curious. "Do you not like going out?"

His smile turned oddly sad. "I do, but…I haven't made that many friends here. I work a lot, for one thing, but the truth is, I'm not always everyone's first choice for company."

"Is this a necromancer thing again?"

"Yes. And I don't want to sound like I'm fishing for pity. I'm not. I love my life, love my work, which might sound like a funny thing to say about making doughnuts, but they make people happy and I like that. I also wouldn't trade my gifts for any others." His forehead creased with deep thoughtfulness. "It's just that sometimes, I feel so isolated because of who I am."

"That's not fair."

He shrugged. "Life isn't fair. But frankly, being lonely sucks."

"You don't have to be lonely anymore." There

were plenty of people in this town with odd gifts. I couldn't understand why anyone would shun him because his specialty was death. He hadn't chosen to be a necromancer. It made me sad for him. It made me want to show him that he had a friend in me.

Maybe more than a friend. I took his handsome, serious face in my hands, the beads in my new bracelet catching the light and sparkling right along with the diamonds next to them. He was warmer than Greyson, but cooler than Cooper. He was just right. I leaned up and kissed him.

He kissed me back, tenderly at first, almost teasingly, but then the intensity increased and his grip tightened on my waist. He tugged me closer, and my hands slipped to his shoulders.

Pleasure spread over me like frost covering a window. I was powerless to stop it. Didn't want to, either. It was too beautiful a feeling.

My head spun with the same kind of happy feeling sugar gave me. I was floating and blissful and, when he finally broke the kiss, panting slightly.

I blinked to clear some of the fog from my head. Sin was still holding on to me. He was breathing openmouthed, his eyes dark and wild. He let go and stepped back, breaking into a big smile. "I should give you a bracelet every day."

I laughed. "I was just trying to make you feel less lonely."

"Job done. And done well." He crooked his arm toward me. "We should go back in. The evening will be winding down soon."

I sighed as I looped my arm through his. "I guess all good things must come to an end."

"Not always." He looked sideways at me. "We could all go out for breakfast."

"Ooo, pancakes."

He laughed. "You have the most impressive appetite of any woman I've ever known."

"Um, two words. Birdie Caruthers."

He held the door for me. "All right, you have the second-most-impressive appetite."

We walked back in, and he slipped his hand in mine. "Is that a yes to breakfast, then?"

I stopped searching the crowd for my mom and aunt to answer. "I'm in, but my mom and aunt Martha probably won't stay. They've already had the sleigh out long enough to make my uncle antsy."

He shook his head. "I still can't believe your uncle is Santa Claus." Then he nodded toward the crowd. "Your aunt is waving at us. We should go join them."

"Let's go."

As we headed toward them, the lights changed and new, smaller snowflakes were projected over the crowd. Then real snowflakes began to fall from the ceiling, and the music softened. The evening was almost over. I felt a kinship with Cinderella at that moment, hearing the first strike of the clock at midnight and knowing that everything was coming to an end.

I'd get to see Sinclair again, but he was only one part of this magical night. Having my mom and aunt here had been the best. I hugged them both as we joined them.

"What was that for?" my mom asked.

"I just love you guys. And I'm really glad you came." The snow was coming down harder now. Elenora must have told Lark to ramp it up to get people out.

My aunt smiled. "Tonight was so much fun, wasn't it?"

"It was." I glanced up at Lark. She was staring straight ahead, eyes narrowed in concentration. Some elves had to work harder to produce the shimmer than others. Shimmer was a term winter elves used to refer to this particular kind of snow magic. It was the same thing we did in the stores on Snowy Saturdays. The snow was real, but magical, so once it fell, it disappeared, leaving no puddles or trace behind.

"Oh my, that's a lot of snow," Aunt Martha said.

I looked down at my feet. This magical snow that was supposed to be disappearing wasn't. It was piling up. Everywhere. There had to be a good four inches on the ballroom floor. "What in the name of Christmas is Lark doing?"

"I can't imagine," my mother said.

"No way Elenora asked for this." My breath spilled out of my mouth like smoke, instantly turning to vapor in the air. I hadn't noticed the drop in temperature, because winter elves didn't feel the cold like other supernaturals.

Sinclair must have, though. I checked to see if he was shivering. He wasn't. He wasn't moving at all. I put my hand on his arm.

He was frozen. And the snow was falling so thickly that visibility was limited to a few feet.

"Son of a nutcracker." I tried to turn around to see the rest of the crowd. My feet wouldn't budge. "Mom, Aunt Martha, do something."

They didn't answer me. They were frozen too.

Ice climbed up my body, solidifying each limb until I was a giant elfy Popsicle. Then the frost covered my eyes and filled my ears, cocooning me in snow. I couldn't see, couldn't hear, couldn't move, couldn't get a sound out that wasn't muffled by the snow. I was a prisoner.

Of my very own brand of magic.

As I struggled to free myself, I was vaguely aware of movement and the cracking of ice. I felt some pressure on my throat and wrists but it was gone as soon as I'd felt it. Then, a few seconds later, the ice and snow were gone without a trace, and I was frozen no more. I shook myself, not really sure what had just happened. Freezing a winter elf had to take some strong magic. Outside of my father, I didn't know of any other winter elf who could pull off that kind of stunt without a massive amount of effort. Me, maybe, but I wasn't sure. I'd never tried to freeze another elf.

I looked around. My aunt and mom looked fine, but it seemed like most of the crowd was having a harder time shaking off the cold. A lot of people were shivering and rubbing their arms. Some were stamping their feet and blowing on their hands. The vampires looked more dead than usual. Almost blue from the cold.

But not a drop of water or a single melting flake was anywhere. All traces of our three-second ice age were gone. That's how the shimmer was supposed to work.

"What the devil was that?" Sinclair growled. He was rubbing the back of his neck.

"Bad shimmer," my aunt answered. "That's what that was."

I nodded. "For sure."

I was about to check on Lark to see if she had a clue how badly she'd screwed up when my mother gasped. "Oh, Jayne. Where is your tiara? And your necklace?"

My hand went to my throat. The snowflake necklace with its rare pale blue diamond was gone.

I shook my head. "I have no idea." I stared at her. "Your jewelry is gone too. Aunt Martha, yours too." My stomach coiled into a miserable knot. The pressure I'd felt and the crackling ice I'd heard when frozen made perfect sense now. Both were side effects of my jewelry being stolen.

"Oh no." Aunt Martha looked like she might cry.

"What?" My mother felt the top of her head for her tiara. "Your father is going to—"

An ear-piercing shriek cut her off. "Security! Shut the doors *now*. No one gets out."

The voice belonged to Elenora. We all looked in

her direction. As a horde of security people streamed through the crowd, she strode up to the stair landing and faced the gathering. She was as pale as the snow that had entombed us. The ballroom doors slammed closed.

A new chill, one of my own making, settled over me when I saw the Heart of Dawn was no longer around her neck.

Elenora's fangs were visible and her eyes were glowing. She seemed to be vibrating with anger. I'd never seen her like that. I'm not sure anyone had. "Whoever thinks they can steal from me and get away with it is a fool. With a death wish."

Her grandsons and their partners joined her on the landing, flanking her like the world's scariest group of backup singers. Five vampires and one valkyrie. And they all looked ready to kill. Elenora was right. Whoever had stolen that diamond wasn't going to get the chance to finish their bucket list.

I cleared my throat, then called out to her. "Elenora."

She looked at me, relaxing a tiny bit. "What is it, Princess?"

"All of our jewelry has been taken as well. Mine, my mother's, and my aunt's."

Her eyes widened in shock, then her anger returned. She scanned the crowd. "Who else had jewelry taken?"

A scattering of hands went up.

Elenora looked my way again, the glow in her eyes a little unnerving. "The snow and ice that fell on us is winter elf magic, is it not?"

I nodded. She couldn't possibly think any of us had been involved, could she? After all, the three of us had been ripped off too. "It is."

Elenora's jaw tensed for a second, then she stabbed a finger toward the balcony and barked a command at the nearest security officer. "Arrest the DJ."

I sucked in a breath and followed Elenora's finger to Lark, along with everyone else in the ballroom. Lark was in her booth looking about as terrified as a person could without crying. Lance was backing away from her.

She shook her head so vigorously her whole body shook. "I didn't do anything. Something went wrong with my magic, that's all. I didn't mean to make so much snow. I just—I couldn't stop it."

Two security guys grabbed her and pulled her out of the booth. Lance got even farther away from her. She disappeared from view for a moment, then appeared again as they hauled her down the stairs. By then, she was crying. "Lance, help me."

He just stared at her, blank-faced with shock.

"I didn't do it, I swear." The air around her turned to ice vapor, melted away, then froze over again. She was radiating cold because she was petrified.

I didn't blame her.

Sheriff Merrow now stood at Elenora's side. His mask was off. He was saying something, and she was nodding. Lark was handed over to him. I expected him to put her in cuffs, but I guess he didn't carry them when he wore a tux.

"How could she?" my mother whispered.

"We don't know that she did it, Mom." Why I was defending Lark I wasn't sure. Except that I really wanted Lark to be innocent since I had basically told Elenora to go ahead and hire her for this gig. Snowballs. This was awful.

Sheriff Merrow raised his hand and addressed the crowd. "Listen, folks. I understand tempers are high, but we aren't going to falsely accuse or arrest anyone. We will be talking to everyone, but until we have some hard evidence, that's all we're going to be doing."

So much for Lark ending up in cuffs. A few groans and protests went up from the crowd.

My mom looked at me. "Honey, if the royal jewels aren't returned to us immediately, what happened here tonight is only a fraction of what your father will do to this town. It will freeze over like a new ice age has hit."

"You have to keep him from doing that."

"I can try, but you know your father."

I did. He could occasionally have a temper. I bit my lip. "I just can't believe Lark would be dumb enough to steal from the woman who hired her."

"How else could it have happened?" Sinclair asked.

"No idea." I glanced at him. He looked paler than usual. "Are you okay? Have you warmed up?"

"I'm fine." He grabbed my hand. "Hey, they took your bracelet too. The diamond one and the one I gave you."

"Aw, man." I looked at my bare wrist.

"They must have broken it when they yanked it off." He gestured toward the hem of my dress. Three rainbow obsidian beads were nestled in the snowflake embellishments near the bottom of my gown.

I carefully freed them and tucked them into my evening bag. Then I studied the little purse as a new thought occurred to me. "Why didn't they take our purses? Whoever they are."

Aunt Martha tucked her evening bag securely under her arm. "I don't think it was a they. I think it was a she."

Which was probably what everyone else thought too. That Lark was the thief. "Maybe Lark did it—she was certainly responsible for the shimmer that froze us all. But there's no way she had the time and energy to do that and run through the crowd taking the jewels. We were only frozen for a few seconds."

My mother frowned. "Jayne's right. Maintaining

that level of shimmer would make doing anything else almost impossible. Someone else must have done the stealing. Another supernatural, based on the speed necessary to strip off that much jewelry in such a short period of time."

I nodded. "We need to explain that to the sheriff. But again, why not take everything? Like our purses. And the men's watches. There have to be some pricey timepieces in this crowd."

Sinclair pulled his tux sleeve back. "You're right. My watch hasn't been touched, and it's worth a good bit. Nothing like your tiaras or necklaces or bracelets, though. Which means they only went for the big-ticket stuff. Elenora's diamond. All of your royal jewels."

He glanced around. "Judging from who else seems to be missing things, it's the same across the board. And they knew what was what. None of the women wearing costume jewelry seem to have lost a single piece."

He was right. There was still plenty of sparkle to be seen in the ballroom, but it was all fake. Rhinestones and crystal and glass. With a sigh, I put my hand on his arm. "I hate to ask, but how much was that bracelet you gave me worth?"

He took my hand. "Willa Iscove made it for me for less than a hundred dollars. All I can think was that the thieves thought it was valuable because you were wearing it. More likely it just got broken while they were grabbing your diamond bracelet."

The ballroom doors opened, and a handful of deputies entered, then the doors were shut again. One of the deputies who'd been at the ball was already talking to Lance. He looked pretty broken up, but then I imagined seeing your girlfriend hauled out of the DJ booth could do that to a person.

Sheriff Merrow held his hands up to quiet the crowd. "I and my deputies will be coming through the crowd to take statements. To make things easier, everyone who had something stolen, please move to the right side of the ballroom. Everyone else, we'll need your name and contact information, then you'll be free to go."

"That's us." I smiled at Sinclair, even though I wasn't really feeling it. "I guess you're going to have to eat breakfast without us."

He snorted. "I'm not leaving you."

My smile got a little more genuine. "You're not?"

He winked at me. "In for a penny, in for a pound." He smiled at my mom and aunt. "Ladies, I'm at your service. Why don't we find a spot for you to sit and wait, and then I'll see about getting you some drinks? Water, coffee, tea, whatever you want."

Aunt Martha smiled. My mother didn't, but she was probably trying to work out how she was going to explain all this to my dad.

"A cup of tea would be divine." Aunt Martha took Sinclair's arm. "Aren't you sweet to offer?"

He was. Very. My mom and I followed him and Aunt Martha to the right side of the ballroom and took some of the chairs Elenora's staff was setting up.

Sinclair stayed standing. "Anyone else want a cup of tea?"

My mother held up her hand. "Nothing for me, thank you."

Nerves had turned my mouth into the Sahara. "I wouldn't mind some water."

"Be right back." He went off in search of those beverages, leaving us to wallow a bit in our craptastic situation.

I snuck a peek at my mom. "I'm really sorry about all this."

She put her arm around me and laughed softly. It was a nice sound to hear in the midst of all this. "Honey, you have no reason to apologize."

"I kind of do. You guys wouldn't have been here if not for me. And I could have told Elenora not to hire Lark."

"But we don't know that Lark had anything to do with this. And that wouldn't have been kind," my mom said. "You weren't raised to be vindictive."

My aunt snorted. "Her father might argue that."

My mom pursed her lips. "Jack's version of

justice might be a bit more stringent than most, but he's not as rash as you make him out to be."

I didn't want to start an argument, but the truth was, my father had a documented temper. I didn't hold it against him. Being king meant dealing with incredible amounts of stressful nonsense at times. Although it was my understanding that he was a lot calmer since marrying my mom.

Instead of saying any of that, though, I sat back and stared up at the ceiling and the rhinestone snowflakes dangling from it. They threw soft sparks of rainbow light, making me think about the bracelet Sinclair gave me, and just like that, I was mad again. I'd had that bracelet less than half an hour and already I missed it more than my tiara. It certainly had more personal meaning. I sighed out a long, frustrated breath.

"It'll be all right, Jay."

I glanced at my mom. "You really believe that?"

"I do." Her gaze was focused on Elenora and the swirl of activity around her. "That woman isn't about to let anyone get the best of her. I just met her today and I know that much about her."

I watched Elenora with her family surrounding her. They seemed serious and focused and like they were already operating with a plan. That was the Ellingham way. They were a family unit. Just like the Frosts and the Kringles. "You're right. This will get solved."

I just hoped they hadn't already decided Lark was guilty. Something about this whole situation didn't sit easy with me. I thought about talking to Elenora about my gut feelings, but then the sheriff approached us.

He nodded at me. "Princess Jayne."

I introduced my mom and aunt to him, then he pulled up a chair to speak to them. "I'm sorry that your first experience in our town had to end this way. I hope you won't hold it against us. We're going to do everything we can to recover your jewelry."

Sinclair came back. He handed my aunt her tea, then sat beside me and gave me a bottle of water. "Everything okay?"

"So far." I cracked the bottle and took a long drink. It wasn't Dr Pepper, but it did the trick.

The sheriff pulled out his notebook. "Lady Kringle, why don't you start? Tell me what pieces were taken and describe them for me."

It took forty-five minutes to get through all three of us. I made sure to tell Sheriff Merrow about each piece, including my obsidian bracelet. When he was satisfied and ready to release us, I had a question of my own for him before he left us.

I stood up. "One thing, Sheriff."

He stopped and turned around. "What's that?"

"I don't see Lark. Has she been taken into custody after all?"

He glanced at my mom and aunt, then back at me. "Not yet. Not enough evidence against her yet."

"If it comes to that, and you do take her in, you know you can't hold her in a regular cell. If her magic is really that powerful, she could freeze those metal bars and snap them like twigs."

He nodded. "We'll be holding her in a private area. Especially for supernaturals."

I knew what that meant. The Basement. The tunnel system that lay beneath the streets of Nocturne Falls. It was more than a tunnel system, though. There were storage rooms, multiple street-level access points, and a place with cells designed to hold all kinds of supernaturals.

"Sheriff." One of the deputies hustled up. Cruz, his badge said. He held up a small plastic bag with a single loose diamond in it. "Found this on the floor in the booth."

Merrow's eyes narrowed. "Go pick her up. Take Blythe."

"Done." The deputy strode off.

"What about Lance?" I asked. "You don't think he's involved?"

The sheriff didn't hesitate. "Everyone's a suspect until they're not, but fae don't have the speed our perpetrator displayed this evening. Doesn't mean we won't talk to him some more."

"Does that mean you're only taking Lark in for now?"

"Yes," the sheriff answered. "I told her and Lance not to leave the apartment they were renting. We should have her in custody in the next few minutes."

"Can I see her? I think she'll talk to me. We've known each other a long time."

His expression didn't change, and he didn't immediately answer.

"I'd consider it a personal favor and promise to do my best to keep my father from freezing the whole town solid when he hears what's happened."

Sheriff Merrow's mouth bent downward slightly. "Five minutes tomorrow morning. Meet me at the station at nine."

"Thank you."

He nodded once. "Now go home. Before I change my mind."

My mom and aunt left right from Elenora's since the sleigh was there, and I promised to send the rest of their things back to the North Pole through the Santa's Bag as soon as I got home. Wasn't like there were any jewels to worry about anymore.

Sinclair and I said goodbye to them, then got into the limo. Elenora had given us each one of the decorated pumpkins to take home after I'd commented on how pretty they were. (My attempt to make her feel better, I suppose, and her attempt to do the same for me.) I put mine on the seat next to me. Sinclair put his on the floor. As soon as the door was shut, he leaned forward. "I need to tell you something, but it has to stay between us."

"Okay. What is it?"

"I touched one of them."

I squinted at him. "The pumpkins?"

"No, one of the thieves. Or *the* thief."

"You—how do you know—can you maybe back up?" I wasn't sure where to start. That was a pretty big statement. "And why didn't you say something sooner?"

He stared at his hands for a second. "I didn't want to have this conversation in front of everyone, because it means explaining one of my scarier gifts. And this isn't one of those things I share with anyone, but these are extenuating circumstances."

Now I leaned forward. "Go on."

He was quiet a second more before he raised his head to answer me. "My touch can re-animate the dead, but with focus, it can also cause death. Not in the way a reaper can. Mostly in a very localized way. Enough to leave a mark. A mark that could be fatal if left to spread."

Death touch. Noted. "And you touched whoever took the jewelry?"

He nodded. "When the ice took over, I was frozen with my hands out at my sides. Whoever grabbed your jewelry brushed by me. Right against my hand. I'd been trying to free myself by pushing power through my fingers. I thought maybe I could kill the ice off in some way. But I know they made contact with me. And I know what my gift does. Somewhere on the thief's body is a spot of death. It'll show itself like a bruise, but it'll be black and wrinkled and it won't heal. The only way to get rid of it is to cut it out. And it will have to be cut out, or whoever bears the mark could die."

I sat back. "Whoa. That's intense."

He stared at his hands again. "I understand if this changes things."

"It certainly does change things. It means we can find out if Lark is the actual thief or not. Doesn't mean she's not guilty of being involved, but it's a start."

He glanced at me. "I meant I'd understand if it changed things between us."

I tipped my head. "In what way?"

He let out a soft breath and looked away for a second before making eye contact again. "Jayne, my touch can cause death. That doesn't bother you at all? You who were just in my arms earlier?"

"You said it takes concentration. Have you ever done it accidentally?"

"No, but it's still a part of who I—"

"You realize what happened tonight was winter elf magic. That I'm capable of the same thing Lark did tonight. More, really, because I'm a direct descendant of Jack Frost. And my father's powers are a magnitude higher than anything you saw tonight."

"But what happened tonight takes a lot of work, right? Real concentration."

"Depends. You know what doesn't take a lot of work? Making a deadly blade that will melt away into nothing." I held my hand out and produced a dagger made of sparkling, crystalline ice. "I can make them in any shape. Any size." I changed the dagger into a cutlass, brandishing the short sword with a twirl of my wrist. "The perfect murder weapon. If that doesn't freak you out, then I think we're good."

"But ice isn't strong enough to kill someone with. It doesn't have the tensile strength."

"Magically produced ice isn't like an icicle off the roof." I picked up my pumpkin by the stem and held it away from me. I sliced it cleanly in half with the cutlass. Then I opened my hand and let go of the blade, using a little extra magic so that it melted before it hit the carpet, leaving no trace. "See what I mean?"

His eyes were a little rounder as he nodded. "Point made." Then he smiled. "And no, I'm not freaked out by that. Completely impressed, though."

"As you should be." I laughed as I looked at my pumpkin. Then I sighed. The bright orange insides looked like a crime scene against the bedazzled white exterior. And there were pumpkin guts on the limo carpet. "Snowballs. I was going to put that in the shop window."

"You can have mine."

That made me smile. "Are you sure?"

"Elenora only gave it to me because you said

you liked them." He side-eyed his pumpkin. It was covered in alternating stripes of clear and white iridescent crystals. "Does that look remotely like something a shop called Zombie Donuts would display?"

I laughed. "Not really. But mine might work."

He chuckled. "True."

I leaned back and stared out the window. "Back to this mark for a second. I don't think Lark's just going to voluntarily take off all her clothes. How am I going to find out if she has a death mark on her?"

Sinclair thought about that. "My hands were a little higher than my waist. How tall is Lark?"

"A little shorter than me."

"If she was going straight past me, the mark should be on her arm just above her elbow. Or it might be on her rib cage if she was turned. All she'd have to do is lift her shirt up. Either way, it won't be hard to spot."

"Are you sure her brushing by you would be enough? Do your gifts work through clothes?"

"Yes and yes. With as hard as I was focusing my power in an attempt to get rid of the ice, there's no way the thief got by me unscathed. And really, you should be able to tell even without seeing the mark. I understand they're very painful."

"Okay, that sounds like enough for me to go on." I blew out a breath. "Some night, huh?"

167

"That's for sure." He glanced at his watch. "We still have time for pancakes."

"What time is it? Mummy's doesn't open until six. And what do you mean we still have time?"

"It's almost two in the morning. But my day starts at four A.M. No need for Mummy's, though. I'll make the pancakes."

"You start work at four in the morning?" That was a somewhat horrifying thought. At least for a person like me, who enjoyed sleep like a winter elf liked cake. And by winter elf, I meant me.

"We open at six just like Mummy's, and those doughnuts have to be ready, so I start early. I have dough to make, some of it has to rise and proof, there are fryers and ovens to turn on so they can come to temperature, glazes, fillings, and toppings to prepare. Lots to do." He grinned. "You didn't think I had a shop full of doughnut-making fairies, did you?"

"No. I guess I just never thought about how much work it is. Don't you want to sleep a little before you have to do all that?"

"Not if it means missing breakfast with you. Plus, I can nap after the morning rush is over. My employees are perfectly capable of handling the rest."

As much as I loved and needed my sleep, I knew I was too wound up to drift off right now anyway. "Okay. Pancakes it is."

Smiling, he leaned back and rapped on the glass divider between us and the driver. The window whirred down, and Sinclair gave the guy the change of address.

Twenty minutes later, I was wearing a pair of Sinclair's pajama pants and a Zombie Donuts T-shirt (and my strapless bra, which I'd be tearing off the minute I got home), sitting at his kitchen counter and watching him make huge, fluffy pancakes. It shouldn't have been a surprise that he could make pancakes, what with all his doughnut skills.

His apartment was above his shop, just like Willa lived above her jewelry store. It was a cool setup, and I liked that the Ellinghams had thought about stuff like that when they'd rebuilt the town. Or maybe I was biased because I lived in an apartment above my store, too.

Either way, his place was nice. Lots of wood and leather like you might expect in a man's home, but also a surprising amount of glass and art and plants. It felt very metropolitan to me. Like an apartment you might see in a chic new neighborhood in a big city. I liked it. His cat, Sugar, was sitting on the back of the sofa, watching us. She was a gorgeous little creature with big gold eyes.

Sinclair had changed into pretty much the same outfit as he'd given me, but the pajama pants and T-shirt looked a lot better on him. He glanced in my direction, spatula raised. "I could throw some blueberries in these. Or chocolate chips. Or butterscotch chips. Or coconut. Or—actually, I could put pretty much anything you want in these. The shop is full of stuff we could add in."

"I'd be perfectly happy with plain. With syrup, of course." He was already going to enough work, and who didn't love regular pancakes?

"Of course." He put the spatula down to retrieve a jug of maple syrup from the refrigerator.

There was a Canadian flag on the jug. That meant it was the good stuff. "That will do nicely."

He set it on the counter beside the butter. "You want coffee?"

"I'm torn. Part of me thinks I should avoid the caffeine so I'll be able to sleep, and part of me thinks sleep is just a dream." I snorted. "No pun intended."

He snorted. "You should skip it. No point in disrupting the few hours of sleep you're going to get." He went back to the griddle, checking the edges of the pancakes.

A phone buzzed.

He looked up. "Is that you or me?"

I glanced over my shoulder. My evening bag was about to vibrate off the coffee table. Sugar was giving it the side-eye. "Me." I scooped it up and pulled the phone out. There was a text from Greyson.

Complication with the job. Won't make it back for another day. Sorry. Hope you had fun at the ball.

That explained why he hadn't shown up. *I did. Lots to tell you when you get back. Be safe.*

"Everything okay?" Sinclair asked.

"Yes." I tucked the phone away. "Just a friend checking in."

"If you need to make a call and want some privacy, you can use the bedroom."

As tempting as it was to see what Sinclair's bedroom looked like, I had no reason to. "No, it's fine." I came back to my seat.

He slipped an enormous pancake onto my plate, then put one on his, added two more to the griddle and came around to join me while they cooked.

We slathered the pancakes in butter and syrup. I finished before he did, happily stuffing the first bite in my mouth. "Hey, these are really good for plain pancakes. They don't taste plain at all."

"Thanks. It's the vanilla. I use really good vanilla. And I add a few drops of almond extract. Not enough to make them taste like almond, but enough to give them another layer of flavor."

"No wonder your doughnuts are so good." He and Delaney could rule the world if they ever collaborated.

He finished his bite, got another one on his fork, but then didn't eat it. "You think Lark is guilty?"

"I don't know. I really don't."

171

"Is she capable of doing something like this? I don't mean physically. I mean is this kind of behavior in her nature?"

"I think it could be. I never would have thought so until what happened in college. That upended everything I thought I knew about Lark. She claims to have changed now, but how do I really know that?"

"You can't, I guess. Not with your mutual past."

I sighed. "It certainly doesn't help."

"Do you want her to be guilty?"

I glanced at him. That was a loaded question. "No. I definitely don't. I'd like to find out she really is a different person. But, man, things don't look good for her, do they?"

"No, they don't."

"I'm in such a bad spot with this." I stared at my pancake. "I could have kept Elenora from hiring her, but I didn't. I basically gave Lark my blessing. So if she did do this, it's partially my fault."

"Elenora won't hold that against you." He hesitated. "Will she? I haven't been here long enough to know her well enough to really say that."

"You saw her at the ball tonight. Did she look like the warm, forgiving type to you?"

"Not exactly, but you can't be held responsible for someone else's actions."

I ate another bite. "I hope not."

Several hours later (not enough of which had been spent sleeping), I was walking into the sheriff's department, and I still didn't know what to think about this whole mess. The best I could hope for was that Lark would talk to me and show me she didn't have the death mark on her.

The worst would be if she did.

I fidgeted with the straps of the tote bag over my shoulder. Either outcome would lead to more questions, more accusations, more problems. But her not having the mark meant I would be free and clear. Well...sort of. Just because she didn't have the mark didn't mean she might not have been working with someone.

Snowballs.

Birdie greeted me with a smile that held a large amount of pity. "You okay, Princess?"

"As okay as I can be." I reached into the pocket

of my jacket and used the tips of my fingers to spin the obsidian beads on the safety pin I'd hooked to my keyring. I hadn't wanted to lose them or leave them behind, and I was mad about the bracelet being broken, so I'd figured out a way to keep them with me. It felt like righting a wrong. "All things considered."

"Sure, sure. How are your mom and aunt?"

"Good, I guess. I haven't talked to them since they got home." I'd purposefully avoided the snow globe this morning, although I had put their luggage into the Santa's Bag and sent it back to the North Pole. That was about all I'd gotten accomplished.

I'd had roughly four hours of sleep, and I was feeling it. Talking to my dad about what had happened last night was super low on my list of things to do. At least until I had spent some time with Lark and hopefully had more answers.

"You want anything? Coffee? Cinnamon roll?" Her smile widened. "I'd offer you some doughnuts, but I'm guessing you've had quite a lot of those lately."

Sheriff Merrow came out of his office in time to hear his aunt's comment. "Leave the girl be, Birdie. She's got enough on her plate."

"That's for sure," Birdie said. "And some of it's doughnuts."

"Aunt Birdie." He narrowed his eyes.

I snorted despite myself.

She held her hands up. "Just trying to lighten the mood."

He sighed. "Try doing that filing I left on your desk instead."

With a hmph and a glare at him, she picked up a stack of files and marched off to the back room.

He turned his attention to me. "What's in the bag?"

"A change of clothes for Lark. You have any problem with that? It's just sweatpants and a T-shirt." They were my big plan to check her for the death mark, so I really hoped the sheriff allowed it.

He didn't respond for a second. "Fine. But her old clothes leave with you."

"Okay, I can do that, thanks." I hooked my thumb under the strap over my shoulder. These clothes were also my insurance policy against Lark not wanting to talk to me. She'd been in a silk bustier, cropped leather jacket, and leather pants last night. She had to be ready for something more comfortable. Unless she'd changed in the brief time she'd been home before being arrested. Hmm. I hadn't thought about that until just now, but the sheriff didn't seem to think Lark changing clothes would be weird, so she must still be dressed in all that leather.

He just grunted, then said, "Follow me."

I did, and he took me to a door at the back of the station. It was about as nondescript as a closet door, except for the plaque that said Employees Only. He swiped a keycard through the lock to open it, then we went down the steps and came out into one of the main passageways of the Basement. The wide corridor was well lit and very industrial-looking with little directional signs here and there. Just like I remembered it.

We walked along for a bit and came to the holding area. He used his keycard again to unlock that door. When it clicked, he nodded at me. "Five minutes."

That wasn't very long. "What if she starts talking?"

"Keep listening." He opened the door and held it for me.

I took that to mean I'd have more time if I needed it. I hoped that's what he meant. I went inside. The space was bright and clean. Lark was in the last cell on the left. All the cells were fronted in thick plexiglass, but hers had been molded into bars whereas some of the others just had sheets of the stuff with air holes. The door was solid plexiglass, though. Different setups for different supes, I supposed, but I knew enough to know that what looked like plexiglass was most likely something much stronger and magically enhanced to be that way.

She was sitting on a wide, molded bench. Her knees were pulled up to her chest, and her arms were wrapped around her legs, her face down against her knees. Fortunately for me, she hadn't changed her outfit. She lifted her head as I approached.

By her red eyes and smudged makeup, she'd been crying. "Come to gloat?"

"No," I said. "I came to see how you're doing." I took the bag off my shoulder and held it up. "Brought you a change of clothes, too."

She dropped her feet to the floor. "Really?"

"Yes. You want them?"

"Totally." She got off the bench. I realized that the dark circles under her eyes weren't entirely from makeup, but lack of sleep.

"You have to send your old clothes back out."

She nodded. "Okay."

There was a narrow slot in the solid plexiglass door with a little ledge on both sides. I guessed that's where they put food trays through. I stuffed the bag in and took a few steps back. I wasn't about to give her any privacy, though. I couldn't.

She picked up the bag and gave me a cold look. "You just going to stand there and watch?"

There was an almost snarly edge to her voice. I brushed it off. I'd probably react the same way if I was locked up. Short on patience and ready to snap. "Just change already. I only have a few minutes. And it's not like we didn't change in front of each other all the time in college."

She frowned but shucked her jacket. Nothing on her arms, except for a tattoo on her shoulder of a crescent moon.

"What happened last night, Lark?"

"If I knew, I probably wouldn't be in here." She took off her pants next. Peeled them off, really. I guess leather pants worked that way. I'd never worn any, so I had no idea. I didn't think I would be wearing them, either. No marks on her legs. Which wasn't where Sinclair had thought the mark would be anyway.

"I get that. How did your shimmer go so wrong?"

She hitched the sweatpants up and rolled her eyes. "Again, if I knew—"

"You realize I'm trying to help, right?" Lack of sleep and stress had made me a little short on patience too. "I didn't need to come here this morning."

She sighed and pulled the T-shirt on. Over the bustier. Snowballs. She reached up under the T-shirt and started to unhook the bustier. Which was probably what I would have done.

But I needed to see her rib cage. I had to think fast.

She dropped the bustier onto the bench, giving me a glimpse of skin when she tugged it free.

I pointed at her. "Did you have that bruise before?"

She yanked the shirt up, giving me a good look at the front of her. "Where?"

"Other side," I said.

She turned, lifting the shirt again and showing me half her back in the process. "This side?"

Her right was unmarked. "Other other side."

She repeated the move on the left. "I don't see anything."

Neither did I. And she wasn't moving like someone who was in any pain, which she would have been, based on what Sinclair had said about the marks. I shrugged. "Must have been a shadow."

She pushed her clothes piece by piece through the slot, along with the bag. I picked them all up and stuffed them in the bag. "I'll make sure you get these back."

She snorted. "You think I'm actually getting out of here?"

"Why wouldn't you?"

"You heard Elenora last night. All that death-wish talk. She's probably going to drain me dry and leave me for dead."

"I don't think vampires really do that anymore." Although, I wouldn't put it past Elenora to threaten Lark with that.

"Yeah, well, of course you'd think that. They like you. And you like them."

"That's not a crime." That last word hung

between us like a flashing neon sign. "Look me in the eyes and tell me you didn't do it."

She came right up to the bars. "I didn't do it. And I don't know why my magic went wrong."

"What about Lance? How much do you know about that guy?"

"A lot. We've been together for a long time. We love each other. We trust each other. And he was with me all night last night."

"He never left your side?"

"Only long enough to get me drinks and bring me some food. And then he was only gone for as much time as it took to do those things. He's a good guy. A really good guy."

"Has your magic ever gone wrong like this before?"

She sighed and sat on the bench. "Once. But not to this extreme. And it was like a year ago."

Interesting. I leaned against the bars. "What happened?"

"I was tired. The night before, I'd done an extra show because the money was good. I ended up filling half the club with snow. The crowd loved it, but it was definitely a malfunction. I snapped out of it, and the snow disappeared. Just like last night."

"What do you mean you snapped out of it?"

She made a face. "Last night and that night a year ago, both times, it was like I was in a fog. Sort of. It came and went so fast that the memory of it is just a fleeting one."

"Were you under a spell?"

"No. Didn't feel like that. Felt like…being tired."

"Is there any way you could have left the booth while you were doing the shimmer?"

"You mean so I could run around and steal everyone's stuff?" She narrowed her eyes at me. "No. And even if I had, where would I have put it? I'm sure the cops have gone through all my stuff by now anyway. Which is how they found that loose diamond by my gear that isn't mine. The real thief planted that. They had to. Where else could it have come from?"

"Right." I had my doubts about that. I thought through everything she'd said. "Who books your shows?"

"Lance handles all of that."

He was more deeply imbedded in Lark's life than I imagined. I rubbed my forehead. I was going to regret this, I just knew it. "I'll…try to help you."

"You will?" Her hopeful look suddenly turned suspicious. "Why?"

"Because my family's royal jewels were stolen and because I'm partially to blame for you being here." Not because I thought she was completely innocent. I hadn't gone that far down the road yet.

She made a face. "How so?"

"Elenora asked me if you were trustworthy. Told me she wouldn't hire you if I said so."

Lark's lips parted and a soft, "Oh" escaped.

I paced to the other end of the cell. "Don't get all emotional about it. We're still not going to be best friends when this is over. I'm just glad you weren't the one stealing the jewels."

"You seem pretty sure of that." She got up and came to the bars. "Which I'm glad of, don't get me wrong, but why are you so confident about it?"

I wasn't going to tell her about the mark. "Just a feeling. Besides, your parents have money. And you said yourself you're doing all right as a DJ. If you needed money, you could just ask them." Unless they'd cut her off. Which was a possibility. "I also don't think you'd want to jeopardize your career with a stunt like this."

Lark's face was unreadable, then she lifted her chin in an expected gesture of haughtiness. "Look, I appreciate the offer, but I don't want you to put yourself out for me. This is all going to work out. I know it will, because I'm innocent and they're not going to find any real evidence against me."

Now who seemed confident? I changed the subject. "Where's Lance?"

"They picked him up the same time as me. I guess they're holding him too, but since they aren't keeping him here..." She shrugged one shoulder. "Maybe they let him go already."

"Right." I thought some more. "Where in town are you staying?"

"We're renting an apartment on Black Cat Boulevard. It's just down from the coffee shop over there."

"Okay, I'll go over there, see if I can find Lance, and talk to him." If the sheriff didn't still have him locked up. "Maybe he knows something."

"Thank you," Lark whispered. There were tears in her voice.

I wasn't up for that. Not after the night I'd had. It reminded me of how she'd cried with me in college over losing Cooper. And hindsight had proven that to be a big show. Maybe that sounded unsympathetic of me, but I felt like I was walking on thin ice here. Even if she hadn't physically taken the jewelry herself, she was involved in this somehow. She had to be. She'd been right in the middle of it.

Unless I was letting past history cloud my judgment.

"Will you come back and tell me what you find out?" She clung to the bars. "Will you see if they'll let me out?"

"The best I can do is call your parents and ask them to pay your bail. Although I'm not sure we're at that stage yet."

"No." She backed away from the bars. "I don't want them to know about this. Not until they absolutely have to. Tell Lance I'm counting the hours until I see him again."

"Okay."

"Promise me you'll tell him."

"I will. Promise." Although, *ew*. I left and rejoined the sheriff in the hall. "Have you already picked up her boyfriend? Lance? Have you talked to him?"

The sheriff nodded. "He claims he was frozen like everyone else."

We walked back to the stairs that led to the station. "Do you believe him?"

"No."

I glanced at the sheriff. "Are you holding him?"

"For twenty-four hours. That's all the law allows until we have enough evidence to arrest him. Same with Lark."

We started up the steps. "He's at the station, then."

"Yes. And you can't talk to him."

"I wasn't going to ask." I had been, but knew my boundaries with the sheriff. Birdie on the other hand... "Did you search the place where they're staying?"

"Yes." The sheriff stopped at the landing and gave me a frustrated look. "Miss Frost, I realize you have a dog in this hunt, but it's not my first time into the woods. I know how to run an investigation."

I held my hands up. The last thing I needed to do was make an enemy of the law. And his analogy was also a pointed way of reminding me he was a werewolf and very capable of handling a supernatural investigation. "You're right, and I know that. But I can't help myself."

I dropped my hands with a groan. "Elenora hired Lark because of me. So I feel responsible, not just for her diamond being stolen, which is awful, but do you realize some of the pieces my mom and aunt lost have been in our family for nearly a century? They're not just pretty sparkling things, they're Winter Court history."

His expression softened. "I'll do my best to keep you in the loop."

"Thank you."

I skipped attempting to see Lance, instead writing him a quick note with Lark's words, which Birdie promised to deliver. After that, I got back to my office as quickly as possible so that I could talk to my dad. I didn't need him any more wound up than he already was. It took him about half a second to answer the snow globe.

"Are you all right?"

I nodded. "I am. Really upset. But okay. How are Mom and Aunt Martha?"

"The same. Upset. As am I." He sighed, and vapor trails whirled through the air. He was mad, all right.

"I'm really sorry about all this, Dad. I couldn't be more sorry."

"I know you are. And it's not your fault."

"Except it kind of is."

"Jayne. No." He gave me that look that made me feel like I was twelve and had just cut the whisker off of Blitzen. (Yes, reindeer have whiskers.) "I know what you're thinking. Stay out of it."

"But Lark—"

"Is the sheriff's to deal with now." He took a breath. "I realize this is Winter Court business. If Lark perpetrated this crime, I want to know about it so that I can deal with her appropriately, but that doesn't mean you're to involve yourself. Do you understand?"

I slumped in my chair. "Yeah, I get it."

He raised a single blue brow. "I'm serious, Jay. Not only do I not want you putting yourself in harm's way, but I don't want you doing anything to impede the sheriff's progress."

I almost rolled my eyes. "I understand." And I was pretty eager to change the subject. "Are you still sending me some holiday help?"

"Yes, they should be arriving this evening. Vale Bright and Crystal Holliday. Their files should have been sent from personnel last week."

I glanced at the stack of stuff on my desk. "I have them. Somewhere. I've read them. They seem nice. And very capable."

"Their arrival is not an excuse for you to dig into this theft." His gaze narrowed. "Do I need to remind you that the store is just going to get busier?"

"Nope. I'm on top of it. Promise. Love you."

"Love you too, Jay." He hung up.

I sat there for a moment, bummed that my dad was so adamantly against me trying to figure out who'd taken the jewelry. Maybe he was just saying that for my mother's mental health. He had to know Lark's involvement made it impossible for me to stand idly by.

I jumped up. I knew exactly where I was going to start.

I had to promise Birdie a dozen bacon bourbon eclairs from Zombie Donuts, but it was worth it to get the info I needed. Which was the exact location of the apartment Lark was renting.

Originally, I figured I'd just check all the apartments on Black Cat Boulevard, because, how many could there be?

Um, a lot. It turned out to be a much bigger task than I'd anticipated, because as many times as I'd been to Delaney's Delectables, which was across the street from the Hallowed Bean coffee shop (both purveyors of tremendously delicious goods and beverages), I had never really paid attention to much else on that street.

Otherwise, I might have noticed that beyond the first couple of shops, there were four apartment buildings and more apartments over most of the shops.

The only downside to asking Birdie was that she now knew what I was up to. I made her swear she wouldn't say anything to Sheriff Merrow and prayed that was enough to keep it on the down low. I could not risk word getting back to my dad.

What he would do if he found out, I wasn't sure. Come to Nocturne Falls? Not this time of year. Still, the less he knew, the better.

With both Lark and Lance in holding cells, there was no better time to scope the place out. Well, technically nighttime might have been a better time, but I didn't want to wait that long. I dressed in jeans, a T-shirt, and a hoodie in an attempt to look as nonchalant as possible.

I also came in from the other side of the street instead of where Black Cat Boulevard met Main. That way I didn't have to walk by Delaney's. Less chance of being seen and recognized that way, because yes, I was well known at Delaney's.

I'd probably head out on Main, though. That way I could make a stop at Delaney's. I mean, I was in the neighborhood. Seemed crazy not to.

The apartment was okay. It wasn't anything lavish, just a one-bedroom with a small kitchen/living room combination. The furniture was mismatched and well used, but it was a vacation rental, so that wasn't so strange. It did have a few nice features, like brick side walls and hardwood floors and a tiny crystal chandelier in the entrance.

I noticed the chandelier because that's what I was staring at while the dizziness subsided. Using my magic to slide under the door had that effect on me. That particular skill was one inherited from my mom's side of the family. It was the magic my uncle Kris used to gain access to all of the houses he visited on Christmas Eve. And while it was a great skill to have, it was one that, for me, came with side effects.

The crystals acted like prisms, sending out little rainbows of light onto the wall. It was very pretty. And immediately made me want a crystal chandelier in my apartment, but I digress. I got to my feet, shaking off the last of the wobbliness and got started investigating.

Despite the place being furnished, most of the drawers and cabinets held very little outside of the essentials again because it was a vacation rental. No one expected it to be fully loaded, just workable in the short term. That made it easy to search quickly. The bedroom and bathroom would have the most stuff that was Lark's and Lance's, so I saved them for last.

I would take my time in those rooms too, because I *had* the time and I wanted to be thorough. There was no telling if I'd get the chance to return. Unless the sheriff found enough evidence to hold Lance on, he'd be released soon and then he'd be back here.

I assumed he'd stay until Lark could leave, too. But it would be interesting—and telling—if he didn't.

The kitchen wasn't very exciting. Most of the cabinets were empty. The fridge was full of take-out containers. The freezer needed a serious defrosting. There was a pint of ice cream crammed into the small cavern of available space, but the rest was iced over. Mint chocolate chip. Lark had always been a cookies-n-cream girl. Maybe that was Lance's ice cream.

I was about to move on to the bedroom when someone put a key into the lock.

Snowballs.

I did the only thing I could think of. I hid under the bed. My pulse was racing. Getting caught in here would be a very bad thing, especially if it was the sheriff.

The door opened and closed, and whoever was now in the apartment came closer. There was nothing under the bed besides me and a suitcase, so if they looked under here for any reason, I was busted.

Feet came into view. They were wearing those sleek leather European-style athletic shoes, and judging by that and the size, this was a guy. And not the sheriff. Had Lance been released already? That didn't seem like something the sheriff would do. The only other detail I could see was dark jeans. As best I could tell, the guy was looking around. Or just standing there. Hard to say from under the bed.

He walked out and came back dragging a kitchen chair. He put it in front of the dresser, then stepped up onto the seat. Small noises followed. A little squeakiness, sort of. Metal on metal, that much I could tell. And every once in a while, the hiss of a breath being sucked through teeth.

Weirdo.

I thought about using my phone's camera to get a better view, but I was face up under the bed, my phone was in my back pocket, and there wasn't enough room to turn over. I tried sliding it out, but my elbow hit the suitcase. It didn't make much of a noise, but I went utterly still, even holding my breath.

The guy on the chair stopped for a second, then resumed whatever he was doing. A few minutes later, there was another louder, sustained squeak. Like a tight hinge being forced open. More noises, softer ones with some overtones of stiff fabric or heavy plastic.

Something plinked to the floor.

I bent my head to the side as much as I could, but whatever had fallen must have gone under the dresser. Or behind it. Either way, it didn't sound like much.

The softer, original noises returned, then he dragged the kitchen chair back and left.

As soon as I heard the door shut, I wriggled out from under the bed and ran to the window that overlooked the street. I waited there until I saw a man come out of the building. He had on the right shoes and jeans. But he was wearing a ball cap that hid his face and a loose parka-type jacket. It was cool out, but not parka weather. He was deliberately obscuring his identity. The best I could make out was he had dark hair. Not Lance, then. His hair was blue.

I went back into the bedroom and looked up over the dresser. An air vent. He'd unscrewed the vent and taken something out, then put the vent back in place. One of the screws was missing. That must be what I'd heard fall.

There was no doubt in my mind that what he'd taken out of the vent had been the jewels. Had to be. What else could it be? There was no routine maintenance that I could think of that would involve taking an air vent off. And what kind of building super wore fancy leather sneakers?

He hadn't been carrying a package that I'd seen through the window, so he must have tucked it into his jacket. No wonder it had been so oversized.

What now? I couldn't exactly go to the sheriff, tell him I'd been hiding under the bed and was pretty sure the jewels had just been removed from the apartment. All I could do was look for more evidence of who this third person was. And try to figure out if Lance and Lark were both involved or only one of them.

My thoughts were a snarled mess of ideas as I started my search again, but there was no evidence to be found. Nothing that could ID another person, or link Lance and Lark to them. There was nothing to even indicate a heist had been planned.

I was about as frustrated as could be. Finally, I gave up and left. I wasn't happy that I'd struck out. How was I going to clear Lark and get the royal jewels back without a lead to go on?

A few minutes later, I found myself in Delaney's Delectables.

"Hey, Jayne, how are you doing?"

I snapped out of the stare down I was having with a tray of truffles and looked up. "Hey, Delaney. I'm...okay." I was miserable, but she didn't need to hear that.

She frowned. "Oh honey, you don't look okay at all."

I tried to smile. I didn't think it worked. "It's such a mess."

"I know." She pushed something into my hand. "Try this, maybe it'll take your mind off things for a little bit."

I looked down at the gold-foil candy cup in my hand. It held a bumpy chocolate ball. "What is it?"

"Pumpkin pecan pie truffle."

That didn't sound terrible. I took a bite. "Mmm,

that's good." My smile came a little easier this time. "Thanks."

She nodded. "This is all going to work out, you'll see."

"I hope so." I ate the other half and talked with my mouth full, which wasn't polite, but I was sort of past caring. "Do you think Elenora blames me?"

"What?" Delaney blinked at me in shock. "No way."

I swallowed. "Are you just saying that to make me feel better? I can take the truth."

"No, I promise, she doesn't blame you. She blames whoever did this."

"Okay." I shifted my gaze back to the glass case of goodies. "But I still think I'm going to need some stuff to get me through this."

She grinned. "You got it. And it's on the house."

"No, it's not. You don't have to do that, and I don't want you to, really."

"How about I just throw in a few extra pieces?"

"I guess that couldn't hurt."

"Excellent. What can I get you?"

I returned to my office with two shopping bags' worth of chocolate, cookies, brownies, blondies, and one mini-cake. Which I would probably be eating for lunch. I restocked the break room with the contents of one bag, then decided two of the boxes of goodies from the other bag would be gifts for the incoming holiday help.

I opened my office door, flipped on the light, and let out a small yelp. Greyson was on the love seat. "What are you doing here?"

"That's a fine welcome home." He swung his feet onto the floor. "But considering what happened last night, I can imagine you're a bit on edge."

"You heard?"

He nodded as he got up. "I'm really sorry, Jayne. I should have been here."

I put the shopping bag on my desk. "It wouldn't have helped. The room was full of supernaturals, and every single one of us was frozen, including the vampires. If we winter elves couldn't break free of the ice, there was no way anyone else was going to." Except for Sinclair, who'd at least freed his fingers.

Greyson hugged me, and it was nice. I stood in his arms for a few long minutes, inhaling his cinnamon scent. Sinclair smelled like doughnuts. "How was your trip?" I mumbled against his shirt.

"It was long. And a little harrowing. But the job was completed without any fatalities, so I'm calling it a win."

"That sounds so cryptic." We separated, and I went to my desk. I was eating some of that chocolate immediately. "What exactly were you doing in Rome?"

He sat back down on the love seat. "I can't talk about it. But I can talk about Lark and the theft all you want."

Greyson not being able to tell me what he'd been up to would have frustrated me on any other day. Today, I had enough to think about already. I opened the box and grabbed a chocolate rum ball. I bit it in half. "I don't even know where to start. I went to see Lark this morning, and based on what I found out, I don't think she did it. But I do think she was involved. Wittingly or unwittingly. But I have no real way to determine that. And I'm not supposed to get involved, per my dad and the sheriff."

"Like that could stop you."

"Exactly." I ate the other half of the rum ball.

"You think it's the boyfriend?"

"Could be. But…" I told him about my trip to the rented apartment.

He scooted forward on the love seat. "So there's a third guy."

"Yeah, and what really sucks is I'm sure he took the jewels out of that apartment while I was there. And I did nothing."

"What could you have done?"

"Frozen him." Why hadn't I done that? I sighed. I'd been so concerned about not being discovered.

"You really think that would have worked based on what happened at the ball? You don't know what kind of supernatural you're up against here. I'm glad you didn't. He could have hurt you. Or worse."

I frowned. Greyson's concern was sweet, but it wasn't really making me feel any better. I went in for a second truffle.

Greyson put his feet on the coffee table. "How could Lark's powers have gone so awry just from being tired? Has that ever happened to you? I would think her powers would be less responsive when tired, not more."

I nodded and thought about that. "My powers have never malfunctioned, tired or otherwise. It makes no sense." I took a hard look at him. "You can't tell me anything you did in Rome?"

He shook his head. "It wasn't a sightseeing trip."

"You seem tired."

"I am."

"And yet, you came here first. That was sweet. Are you going home to get some rest now?"

He tipped his head back and stared at the ceiling for a second. "I wish. Lucian has a new assignment for me already."

"You're leaving again?"

"No, it's a local thing. Apparently, while I was gone, three tourists who'd gone to Insomnia all had their rooms robbed, and Lucian wants me to—"

"Wait. All of those tourists had gone to Insomnia?"

"You know about this?"

"Birdie mentioned it when she told me about Lark DJing at Insomnia, which I don't love, by the way."

"I understand. I didn't mean for that to happen."

"I know and it's fine. Anyway, Birdie didn't say all the victims had been to Insomnia. Makes sense, though, since she did mention they were all supernaturals. She must not have known they'd all been in the club. Have you added that to the report?" Greyson worked as a part-time deputy, basically on an as-needed basis. He also filled in as the Vampire On Duty. When he wasn't running super secret missions for Lucian, of course.

"Not yet. I really did come here straight from the airport."

I looked around the office. "Where's your bag?"

"I left it right inside the warehouse door. You had to walk right by it."

"Huh. Didn't see it. Shows you how preoccupied I am. But listen, back to Lark working at Insomnia while you were gone."

Greyson's brows bent. "Yes?"

"Can you find out what nights she DJed there? We could see if the robberies happened then or at another time. Could help us tie her to something."

"Or the boyfriend."

"Right." Because one of them, or both more likely, had to be involved in this. I couldn't figure it any other way. And if that was true, Lark had played me. Again.

Greyson stood. I'd never seen him look so weary. "I'll head over there now. I need to give Lucian the full report anyway. He doesn't like to do that sort of thing over the phone or email."

"Can't you even give me a hint about what you were doing over there?" I got to my feet, sensing he was about to leave.

Greyson's half-smile seemed to border on frustration. I guess he was done talking about Rome. "Sorry, Jay. No can do."

He put his hand on the door knob, then stopped. "Almost forgot." He took something from his pocket and handed it to me. "I didn't have time to wrap it. I hope you like it."

It was a picture frame no bigger than a business card with a tiny kick-out stand on the back. The frame was covered in a pattern of vines and leaves all done in the smallest mosaic tiles I'd ever seen. It was clearly an antique and expertly done. "It's beautiful. Thank you."

He smiled. "I thought you could put a picture of Spider in it." He leaned over and kissed me. "Talk to you soon, beautiful."

"Get some rest first, okay?"

"Okay." He left, shutting the door behind him.

I put the frame on my desk and sat. My conversation with Greyson had only added more fuel to the fire that was Lark's questionable innocence.

If the tourists who'd had their rooms burglarized had been at Insomnia while the break-ins happened, how could that be a coincidence in light of the robbery at the ball? Also, if Lark was working, she would have been visible the whole time. No way she could have personally done the burglaries. But it remained to be seen if Lance had been with her the whole time at Insomnia or not. And who was this third man?

I had no idea. The only thing I could figure out to do was see if Lance had the death mark on him. How did I get him to take his shirt off? I couldn't exactly bring him clothes the way I had with Lark. Unless new evidence turned up, he'd be released this evening. I guess I could go back to the apartment and try to spy on him…changing.

I shuddered. I wasn't into being a creeper. But I couldn't think of how else to see him shirtless. I groaned and ate another truffle. I really didn't want to spy on Lance. What I wanted was for the sheriff to get back into that apartment and figure out on his own that there was a third suspect. But how? Would seeing the missing screw on the air vent be enough for him to dust for prints?

Someone knocked at my door.

"Come in."

It was Juniper. "You okay?"

"Mostly. What's up?"

"Just checking on you. Also found the chocolates in the break room, which are awesome, thank you."

"You're welcome. Hey—" Inspiration struck. "If you knew a good reason for someone to do something, but you couldn't tell them about that reason, how else could you get them to do the thing you wanted them to do?"

Juniper made a face. "Is this some weird new performance report?"

I laughed. "No, just working through some stuff."

Juni stared at the ceiling, eyes squinting in concentration for a few long seconds. Finally, she looked at me again. "Does the answer have to adhere to any moral or ethical codes?"

I was ready for anything at this point. "Nope."

Juni smiled. "I'd lie."

With a soft snort, I shook my head. "I love you."

"I know." She grinned. "Back to work."

She left as I picked up my cell phone and dialed the sheriff's department. Birdie answered. "Nocturne Falls Sheriff's Department. Birdie Caruthers speaking."

"Birdie, it's Jayne. I need to talk to Hank."

"Ooo, good timing, I was just about to call you."

Setting up another breakfast date could wait. "Birdie, I really need to talk to him now."

"See, that's the thing, Princess. He's not here. He and a couple of the deputies just headed back out to that apartment Lark and Lance were renting."

Was the man a psychic werewolf? My mouth fell open. "How come?"

"Well…" The tone in Birdie's voice was a gleeful mix of emotions. It was her standard for when she had a really juicy piece of news. "Lance just ratted Lark out."

"What?" This was nuts. "Tell me everything."

Birdie laughed. "Turns out, he's been her pawn the whole time."

"In what way?"

"Seems she's been using the threat of her magic to force him to steal valuables from people in the crowd at the nightclubs she performs at. She identifies them, then makes Lance do the dirty work. He claims there's a trail of thefts across Europe that coincide with the dates and locations of all the places she's DJed."

"Insomnia," I whispered.

"That's right," Birdie confirmed. "How'd you know that?"

"I just talked to Greyson. So he confessed to stealing all the jewels at the ball too?"

"No, he said she hired another supernatural, one he doesn't know, to handle all that while she froze everyone."

I rolled my eyes. "So what proof is he offering?"

"Well, Lance told us that everything stolen from those tourists, who happened to be at Insomnia the night before they were robbed, is still in the apartment."

That sounded fishy. "How did the sheriff not find it already?"

Birdie cleared her throat, and her voice dropped to a whisper. "Because she hid the stuff in the air vent."

A chill went through me. Whoever had been there had taken that stuff out. The sheriff wasn't going to find anything. But if I told him I'd been there, if I told him what I'd seen, I was going to be in big trouble. With him and my father. Yeti poop. "Why would Lance do that?"

"He brokered a deal. The sheriff offered to release him on his own recognizance after he signs a statement promising to testify. He'll be out as soon as the sheriff confirms what he's told us."

Well, that wasn't going to happen. There wasn't anything to find in that air vent. Although I was sure Lance was eager to get out and get that death mark taken care of. That had to be killing him. Literally. "Um, okay, keep me posted on whatever—"

The squawk of a radio interrupted me, then Birdie followed. "Hang on, Hank's calling in. Lemme put you on hold."

I got up and paced in an effort to shed the nervous energy building up in my system. Was Lance really the kind of guy to be swayed by the threat of magic? I only knew one other fae, Willa, and she was such a strong, independent woman that I'd assumed all fae were like that. Lance, however, was coming off as a big pushover. I mean, why not just leave Lark if he didn't want to do her dirty work? Why come clean about it now?

And really, stealing jewelry? Was that what Lark was about? After all her talk about how music and DJing made her so happy? And with her family's money? Why take such a risk? Was it a thrill thing?

I blew out a long breath. None of it mattered, really, because they weren't going to find anything in that air vent. Mystery man number three had cleaned it out.

Birdie came back on the line. "I better go, Princess. Hank's on his way back with all kinds of evidence for me to catalog."

"All kinds? What does that mean?"

"All the tourists' jewelry, plus the charms that were stolen from Willa's place a year ago, and you're not going to believe this, but there was a Pocket Pet in there too. Didn't y'all have one of those lifted from Santa's Workshop?"

I stopped pacing, a little dumbstruck. "Yes." I had a lot to process. "You're busy. I'll talk to you later. Thanks." I hung up and stared at my phone.

The mystery man hadn't been taking stuff out of the air vent. He'd been putting it in.

Lark was guilty. At least it seemed that way. Or someone was doing a bang-up job of framing her. But the chances of her not being involved were slipping away.

I sat without moving for a while, just letting the idea of her guilt sink in. I don't know how long I sat there, but I couldn't shake the feeling of disappointment. Weird, right? Because of my past with Lark, I didn't expect to feel that way. But I did.

My disappointment wasn't just in her, though. It was in myself. For not seeing through her lies. For not figuring out that she was playing me. Again.

I needed to talk to someone, but I wasn't sure who. Cooper wasn't an option. He was so occupied with his mom (and who could blame him?) that he hadn't been in touch in days. Greyson was probably getting some much-needed sleep. Juniper was busy with work. And I didn't really want to be the one to break this news to my parents.

That left Sinclair. I checked the time. It was nearly lunch. Wasn't that about when he was supposed to be grabbing some sleep himself? I couldn't bother him.

Which left me feeling pretty alone. I would have loved to have gone upstairs with my mini-cake and spent the rest of the afternoon snuggled up with Spider, watching dumb movies and stuffing my face.

But I had two holiday employees arriving and more work to do than you could shake an icicle at. I had responsibilities.

With a sigh, I picked up the file on top of the stack next to my computer. My phone vibrated, saving me from these inventory sheets for a second longer.

I saw the caller ID and smiled. "Hey. I didn't expect to hear from you. Did you get all the doughnuts made?"

"I did," Sinclair said. "Got them sold, too. How's your day going?"

"Completely nuts. How's *your* day going?"

"Okay. But it would be better if someone had lunch with me."

I smiled. "Shouldn't you be napping?"

"On an empty stomach? Are you nuts, woman? A man can't live on doughnuts alone. Maybe you can, but I can't. I need a burger. Fries. Possibly a milk shake."

I laughed. Oh, I needed this. Needed him. "Pick a place. I'm there."

"Have you been to Mrs. D's Dairy Barn?"

"I don't even know where that is."

"It's just on the outskirts of town. Between Melworth's Kitchens and More and that old run-down motel."

"The Pinehurst Inn?" I'd heard Birdie talk about it.

"Yeah, that place. You want to try it? It's one of those little drive-in joints. I hear they have outstanding burgers, great fries, and milk shakes as thick as concrete."

"I feel a little like I'm cheating on Mummy's, but getting out of town for a bit sounds perfect."

"Pick you up in ten."

And twenty minutes later, we were standing at the counter of Mrs. D's Dairy Barn, ordering food that came in baskets. The place looked right out of the fifties (which might have been the last time it was painted), and I couldn't have been happier. I scored us a table with an umbrella and waited for Sinclair to bring the food over.

I wasn't in any rush. The day had turned into one of those surprising fall days with lots of sun and enough warmth that you could almost forget summer was over. I just sat there and enjoyed it, trying to forget the hot mess that was currently going on.

It was working too, until I saw Lance getting into a sedan with a takeout bag. I couldn't believe he'd gotten out of the holding cell so quickly. Then I pulled my sunglasses off my head and put them back onto my face for a better look. Hmm. Maybe that wasn't Lance after all. Unless he'd also shaved off his creepy little goatee.

The guy in the car had a couple days' stubble and was paler than Lance. Almost chalky. And he moved like he had arthritis, although he didn't look old enough.

"Here you go. Cheeseburgers, fries, a side of fried pickles, one chocolate milk shake for me, and one Dr Pepper float for you." Sinclair set a large tray of food on the table, momentarily blocking my view while he put my order in front of me.

When he sat, the sedan and Lance's facial-hair-free doppelganger had pulled out of the parking lot. I squinted in the direction the car had gone, toward the Pinehurst. That couldn't have been Lance. Lance had blue hair, that guy's hair was dark brownish. Stress was messing with my head.

I smiled at Sinclair and decided to focus on the moment and the company and nothing else. "This looks awesome. Thanks for bringing me here. I needed this."

"I thought you might." He kissed me, something

I hadn't quite expected, but it sure helped me forget about Lark and Lance and all that missing jewelry for a couple of hot seconds. I kissed him back a little, laughing as we broke contact.

"What's so funny?"

I shook my head and picked up a fry. "I like you. A lot."

His grin took over his whole face. "I feel the same way about you." He ate a fry. "Now tell me what's going on, because until now, you haven't been the Jayne I'm used to since I picked you up. Something's bothering you."

"You're sure you want to know?"

"Dead sure."

We ate, and since he'd asked, I told him about everything that had happened.

"Of course you're disappointed. You'd started to think she'd changed. And she hasn't. You put faith in her. And you were let down, again. It's a repeat of college. You have every right to feel blue about it."

"That's exactly it. But talking about it has helped. A lot. Thanks."

"You're welcome." He wiped his hands on one of the paper towels from the roll at the table. These burgers were delicious, but messy. "You think they've found the jewelry yet? Your jewelry and Elenora's, I mean."

"I don't know. I haven't heard my phone yet,

and I'm sure Birdie will call me when they do. If not, I'll call when I get back to the office."

"Lark can't have fenced those pieces already. They're too special. Too high end."

"She could have had buyers in place already."

"True." He ate another fry. "But how would she have gotten them out of town? She's been in a holding cell this whole time."

"Except for between the time she left the ball and her arrest."

"So she had what? Forty minutes A little more? I don't think that's enough time to do anything much."

"She could have dropped the jewels somewhere." I picked a sesame seed off the bun.

"Maybe. But would she really leave that much jewelry just sitting somewhere? Would you?"

I thought about that. "No. I'd leave them with someone. Which is what she might have done too."

"You think there's someone else? You mean Lance?"

I hadn't told Sinclair about the third guy yet, but I'd told him the rest, so why not? Plus, he'd trusted me with the info about his death touch. "Not exactly..." While we finished our meals, I explained what I'd seen and heard at the rental apartment.

His eyes widened when I was done. "Jayne, that was incredibly dangerous of you. I understand why you did it, but I don't like it. Have you told the police?"

"No. Sheriff Merrow told me not to get involved or he'd arrest me for obstruction."

Sinclair snorted. "That man talks a good game."

"Oh, he'd do it all right. It's no game."

"Yes, it is. He's not going to arrest the daughter of the Winter King just to make a point. He was only trying to keep you out of harm's way. For all you know, your father called him and told him to say that."

I stopped with my straw halfway to my mouth. "Son of a nutcracker. That's so something my father would do." And probably had, considering the conversation that had taken place earlier.

Sinclair shrugged. "I'd do it if I was a father and had a daughter to protect. A daughter who's apparently gotten herself into trouble investigating things like this before."

I stuck my tongue out at him. "That'll teach me to share."

He laughed. "Hey, I love your fearlessness, but I'd hate to see you get hurt."

"Thank you." Being around Sinclair made me feel so good.

He yawned and I realized that, while we were having a great time, he needed some sleep. I made a show of checking the time on my phone. "Hey, I should get back to work. My two holiday temps

213

arrive today and I have a lot to do before they get in."

He nodded. "Okay, I'll take you back. Thanks for coming with me."

"Thanks for bringing me." I stood and put all our trash on the tray. "This place was great. And I know you're tired, so it was extra nice of you."

"Happy to do it." He went to dump the trash in the bin.

We grabbed our drinks and walked to the car. He put his arm around me. "I am definitely going to bed when I get home, but if anything comes up, if you need me for anything, you can call me."

"I appreciate that, but nothing's going to come up. It's a done deal."

Except that it wasn't really. When I got into my office, I called Birdie. "Hi, Birdie, I'm sure you're swamped. Do you have a minute?"

"Only just. What can I help you with, Princess?"

There was more noise than usual in the background. "Did Elenora's diamond show up in the air vent stuff? Or any of my family's jewelry?"

She sighed, giving me the answer I'd been dreading. "No. I'm really sorry."

And I was really angry. "Did the sheriff ask Lance about that? I thought he was turning Lark and the goods over in exchange for his freedom?"

"Hank did ask him. Lance said the big pieces were left behind in the DJ booth and that Lark had arranged for them to be picked up by someone else. All he knew was that person was a woman. Another winter elf. Nothing more."

"How is that possible? The deputies searched the DJ booth, didn't they? And the only other female winter elves at that party were me, my mother, and my aunt. And Juniper."

Birdie hesitated. "I know, Princess."

The tone of her voice was very unsettling. "Come on, Birdie. Obviously, my mom and aunt aren't suspects. And I've known Juniper long enough to know there's no way…wait, is Lance claiming *I'm* involved? Why on earth would I steal my own jewelry? I was frozen just like everyone else. He's lying. I had nothing to—"

"Hank sent a deputy to search the DJ booth again."

"And? Because it sounds like there's more."

"He found a secret compartment in one of the lighting boxes. There was a loose diamond in it. One that looks like it came from Elenora's necklace. Just like the one they found on the floor."

I didn't know what to say for a second, then my words returned. "Am I a suspect?"

Birdie swallowed audibly. "Not at this time."

My heart sank. I knew Birdie was only doing her job, but those words cut through me like an ice blade. "That's so reassuring."

"I'm sorry, Princess. I really am, but I can't say

anything more than that about an ongoing investigation."

Well, that was a change. Hank must have put the fear of Jack Frost into her too. "What time was Lance released? Can you at least tell me that much?"

"He's still here. He hasn't been feeling well. He had some kind of seizure. There's a paramedic looking him over now."

Maybe the paramedic would find the death mark. At least I knew for sure that wasn't Lance I'd seen at the Dairy Barn. "Can you text me when he does get released?"

"I don't know…you're not supposed to be involving yourself in this."

"Did my father call the sheriff?"

"I'm not supposed to say."

Which was all the answer I needed. Before I could respond, Kip opened my office door, looking frantic. "Birdie, I have to go." I hung up and looked at him.

"You gotta come now. They're taking Juniper down to the station for questioning."

Juniper was already in the patrol car by the time I made it to the register. The deputy, Blythe, was one I recognized. "What charges are you arresting her on?"

"She's only being taken down to the station for questioning," the deputy answered. "She's not being arrested."

"I'll pay her bail. How much is it?"

"Again, she's not being arrested. There is no bail." Deputy Blythe handed me her card. "Have a good day."

"Are you kidding me?" This was a poop storm of yeti proportions. I checked the time, then looked at Kip. "Call Rowley, tell him to come in now." It was only an hour earlier than he was scheduled. "I'm going down to the station."

"You got it, boss." Kip picked up the phone as I left.

I didn't want to take the time to wait on a Ryde and taking one of the company bikes would make texting impossible, so I walked. Half-ran, really. As fast as I could go while tapping out my message to Greyson. *You around?*

I can be. I'm home.

Meet me at the NFSD.

What's up?

It was too long an answer to text and I was almost there. *Need help.* If that didn't get him to show up, then so be it. I wasn't waiting.

I yanked the station door open and strode toward Birdie. "Where is she?"

"Princess—"

"Birdie, Juniper didn't have anything to do with this mess. Nothing." I was being loud and probably a little obnoxious, but I didn't care. "I want to see her now. I'll give another statement if you want. Or you can question me. But she's not involved in this."

The sheriff walked out of the second interrogation room. "Miss Frost."

"What's going on Sheriff? Are you seriously going to believe the word of that guy over Juniper? He's involved. He confessed to it! He's not the patsy he's trying to make you believe he is."

Sheriff Merrow's glare took on the soft glow of his inner wolf, letting me know just how unhappy he was that I'd shown up. I glared right back. He wasn't about to intimidate me. Much. He pointed behind me. "My office. Now."

I waited for him to storm past me before joining him. He closed the door. "You can't do any good here. We're only questioning her."

"She wasn't involved."

"That's what we hope to find out."

I felt like punching something, and that was not my go-to response. Snow started drifting down around me. Which probably wasn't helping my case, but I was ticked off and beyond caring. "At least let me see her."

He sighed. "When we're done."

"Now."

"Miss Frost, this is an ongoing investigation. And you are impeding it. Go home, or I will charge you with obstruction."

I thought about Sinclair's words that the sheriff would never do that. I believed him, but I wasn't willing to test his theory. "Will you at least call me first if you intend to book her?"

He nodded. "If it comes to that. Which it won't, I'm sure."

"I hope not."

He opened the door for me and I walked out as far as the reception area. "Since I'm here, I might as well get that recipe from you, Birdie."

Birdie squinted at me, but the sheriff kept going to the conference room.

As soon as he shut the door, Birdie leaned over the counter, her voice hushed. "What are you up to?"

"Has Lance been released yet?"

"No, but he's about to be."

"Did the paramedics find anything wrong with him, or was he faking for sympathy?" I crossed my fingers that she was about to tell me they'd found a strange, black bruise on him.

"They said there was nothing wrong that they could find, but he was running a slight fever and complaining of some aches." She frowned. "I'll tell you what it is. He's fae and those holding cell bars are iron wrapped in stainless steel. And you know how fae feel about iron."

I did. Thankfully, elves didn't have that reaction to any metal. But I didn't think the iron in the bars was what was causing Lance's health problems. "Yeah, you're probably right. Call me on my cell if anything happens?"

"I will, promise. So long as my nosy nephew isn't around."

"Thanks." I started for the door. Greyson was just coming in. "What's going on?"

"Walk with me and I'll explain."

"Okay." He turned and followed me out. "Where are we headed?"

"Delaney's. I need a stiff shot of sugar." And it was the perfect place to watch for Lance. I was assuming he'd return to the apartment. Where else could he go?

"You look...really mad."

"I am." I wanted to scream and cry and break something. Kind, sweet, peaceful Juniper must be freaking out in that interrogation room. "They picked Juniper up for questioning."

"What?" He stared at me, almost running into a passing tourist. "Are you kidding? Why?"

I explained, but left out the part about Lance being released soon. Greyson knew me well enough that he'd probably figure out what I was going to do next, and I didn't want to listen to yet another conversation about how I needed to be careful and not get involved.

He swore softly under his breath and shook his head. "Juniper would not have had anything to do with this."

"I know that and you know that, but apparently the sheriff doesn't."

He held the door at Delaney's for me. "You can't fault the sheriff for doing his job."

"Really? Watch me."

Greyson scowled like I was being too hard on the man. "Jay, he has to follow procedure."

"Sure." I stared at the chalkboard menu up on the wall.

"What do you want? I'll get it."

"Dr Pepper and a slice of that Cherry Bomb cake."

"Grab a table, I'll be right over."

I found one of the small round tables that let me see down the street. From here, I could watch the door of the apartment building where Lark's rented place was. If Lance didn't come back here, then he was headed out of town. Most likely with the jewels. Wherever the third man had stashed them.

Greyson came over with our sweets. Well, my sweets. All he'd gotten was a black coffee. "What can I do to help?"

I stuck my fork into the cake and took the point off, but waited until I'd asked my question to eat it. "You know anyone who could fence those kinds of big jewelry pieces?"

"No, but I might be able to do some digging."

The cake was incredible. Like Delaney could do anything else. "On the underweb?" It was a shady, hidden part of the internet where immoral supernaturals traded in all sorts of illegal things better left unknown by the nicer part of society.

"Yes."

"Good." I forked up another bite of cake and took a peek at the apartment building. No sign of him. "That's what I hoped you'd say. How soon can you have an answer?"

"I'll do it as soon as I get home. I'll go now if you want. Which I'm sure you do."

I smiled, hoping my grin wasn't full of cake crumbs. "You're the best."

He smiled back and rested one forearm on the table. "How about dinner at Café Claude's tonight, then?"

"I'd love to, but I can't. My temporary holiday help arrives in about an hour, and I have to get them set up. Tomorrow?"

He nodded. "That'll work." He leaned in, kissed my cheek, and stood. "I'll message you as soon as I find something."

"Text me even if you don't. I want to know either way."

"Okay. Will do. Enjoy your cake."

I watched him walk away, because hello, Greyson in jeans was something worth watching, but as he disappeared from view, I refocused on the apartment building. I knew which window it was. There were no lights on, so I was hoping I hadn't missed him. Unless he was in there and hadn't bothered with the lights.

My mood darkened again, but not enough to keep me from eating more cake. I had two bites left when Lance showed up. He was still in his tux, the tie hanging loose around his neck, shirt unbuttoned. Apparently, like Lark, he hadn't changed before getting hauled in. He looked haggard. Pale, except for the dark circles under his eyes, and very much like a man in desperate need of a shower. I had no doubt these were all effects of the death mark.

Which reminded me that I had a desperate need to see him right before he got into that shower. Well, most of him. Frankly, I wasn't remotely interested in anything lower than his belly button. He had to have that mark on him somewhere.

He shuffled to the apartment building door and went inside. I left the cake and my Dr Pepper behind to follow him, but stopped halfway to the building. What did I think I was going to do? I couldn't very well go on up the steps after him.

Think, Jayne. Think. What would Spider do? I almost laughed at that silly question, but the answer was so perfect, I just stared blankly ahead at the surprise of it.

Spider would use the fire escape.

Did this place have one? Most of the older buildings in Nocturne Falls did, like the building that housed Santa's Workshop and the apartments above it.

I walked as quickly as I could without drawing too much attention to myself and went around the corner. A narrow alley allowed for parking and rear entry to the shops on the ground floor.

It also provided access to the fire escapes. None of the ladders were down, which meant I'd have to jump up and grab the one I needed. Not a big deal, given my better-than-human elf abilities, but it would probably make some noise.

Nothing I could do about that, and time was wasting. I took a running start and made the leap. I caught the second-to-bottom rung and pulled myself up. The clang of metal wasn't as loud as I'd anticipated, but I cringed all the same.

I climbed the rest of the way up with careful steps, hoping to be as soundless as possible. The fire-escape landing was at the bedroom window, but also gave a little access to the transom window over the bed. I snuck a peek through the transom and, as I peered in, caught a glimpse of myself in the mirror over the dresser.

I ducked down, freaked out by the unexpected weirdness of seeing my own face looking back at me.

But I'd also seen Lance. He was standing in front of the closet, which put him at a right angle to me. I would have to be extra careful that he didn't see me. Hopefully, the death mark was keeping him out of it enough to be too observant.

I poked my head around again. He already had the tux jacket off and was working on the shirt's cuff links. I held my breath, waiting. He dropped the shirt and I almost groaned. He still had an undershirt on. No black bruises on his arms that I could see.

He reached for the hem of the undershirt, then a

faint chirping turned him toward the bed. He dug around in the tux jacket and pulled out a phone. The window between us did little to mute the words. "Hello? Yes, just got out. I know. *I know.* How do you think I feel? You know this affects both of us." He paused and stared at the ceiling. "No, not as much as you, but I'm still out here in the public eye."

Was he talking to the mystery man? And what was affecting them?

He rubbed his forehead. "We will. I'll find her and we'll get this sorted, then we'll be on a plane before you know it."

Her? Was there a fourth person involved? Maybe whoever was responsible for selling the jewelry. Lance had told the sheriff there was a woman involved. Another winter elf. Could she be the one who'd produced the shimmer that had frozen everyone? Was the guy I saw at the apartment in the oversized parka actually a woman? None of this was making anything clearer.

He nodded. "Tonight. I promise."

He hung up and tossed the phone on the bed, then scrubbed his hands over his face like he was trying to wake himself up. He groaned and rolled his shoulders. Was he stiff from being in the holding cell or in pain? I couldn't tell.

Finally, he grabbed the undershirt and eased it

off. Nothing on his rib cage or stomach. He tossed the shirt onto the bed with the rest of the clothes and walked out. He passed the dresser mirror as he went, giving me a complete view of his torso.

There wasn't a mark on him.

Anger wasn't an emotion I spent a lot of time with. Sure, I got angry, but I didn't wallow in it. Until today. Today I felt marinated in it. I had to struggle to keep a smile on my face and the edge out of my voice as I welcomed the holiday help.

Vale and Crystal were good elves. They were store openers (they'd actually opened this store), had tons of experience, and having them here was going to make things a lot easier, especially now that we were going to extended holiday hours.

I took them upstairs to the large two bedroom apartment on the third floor the company held in reserve for corporate visits and these kinds of occasions. I gave them a brief tour, then turned over the keys. I realized that my grumpiness was probably evident and that I should explain. "I'm sorry if I'm in a bit of a bad mood. There's a lot going on."

Crystal nodded. "We heard. Don't worry about it. If there is anything we can do to help, just let us know."

"I appreciate that. I really do. Just having you here to help in the shop and with all the new inventory is going to be great."

"What do you need done?" Vale asked. "I'm happy to work this evening if you want me to."

"No, tomorrow's fine. Buttercup and Rowley can handle things tonight. You two get settled in, and we'll get you going in the morning. Crystal, you're on day shift, Vale, evenings."

"Sounds good," he said.

Crystal gave me a little wave. "See you in the morning."

With that handled, I headed back to my office. My phone vibrated with a text. It was from Greyson. He hadn't found a thing on the underweb. So much for that. I thanked him for checking, then called Birdie to find out what was happening with Juniper.

"Hi, Princess. Nothing new to tell you, which is what you called to find out, I'm sure."

"So Juniper is still being questioned?"

"Yes." Birdie sounded apologetic, but I was so upset that only having Juniper back would make things right. "I'm sure it won't be much longer."

I grunted in disbelief.

"Lance is out, though." She lowered her voice.

"Hank had a deputy tail him, and he went right back to the rented apartment."

I already knew that. I just hoped the deputy hadn't seen me spying. "And Lark?"

Birdie sighed. "Lark's been charged with felony theft. I can tell you that much. Elenora's told us to offer her a reduced charge if she produces the jewelry."

I grunted again. "That's not going to happen."

"Why not?"

"Because I don't think Lark has a clue where it is. I'm starting to think she was a pawn in all this. At least to some extent."

"But the evidence at the apartment and the hidden compartment in her lighting equipment all point to her being guilty."

I walked into my office, closing the door behind me. "Makes a good frame-up. That's about it." But I wasn't interested in a big discussion about anything until Juniper was free. "Has my father been notified?"

"We tried, but his cell number just keeps going to voice mail."

"That's electronics in the North Pole for you." And why we used the snow globes. But I wasn't going to share that method of communication with them. The news of Lark being charged could wait. Wasn't like she was going anywhere. "Thanks for the update. I better get back to work."

"You're welcome. Sorry it wasn't better news."

"Me too." I clicked off and sat at my desk, just staring at my computer and the stacks of inventory sheets waiting to be added to the system. I was too angry to work, though. My frustration with Juniper still being at the station was making it difficult to concentrate on anything else.

And then there was Lance. I didn't like the guy. At all. There was something about him that made me want to punch him. He was hiding something. And I wasn't just talking about his involvement in the theft. There was something else going on with him.

Who had he been talking to? And why was he so sick and yet there was no mark on him? I didn't know much about the fae. That was a downfall of mine. I reached into my pocket and pulled out the safety pin holding the three remaining obsidian beans. I'd taken it off my key chain so I could keep it with me more easily. I twirled the beads around as I thought. I knew someone who could tell me more about the fae.

I did a quick search for her phone number and dialed.

"Illusions, this is Willa speaking."

"Willa, hi, you're just who I wanted to talk to. This is Jayne Frost over at Santa's Workshop. Do you remember me?"

She laughed. "Of course I remember you. Hard

to forget the other supernatural royalty in town. Especially when there are only three of us."

I smiled. Willa had abdicated the title of queen to pass it to her sister. I'd heard all about that from Birdie. "Have you talked to Monalisa lately?" I'd only met the Will O'the Wisp once before, but it had been a moment in time that was rather hard to forget. Her then boyfriend had needed help shifting into his true form. A dragon.

"Not lately. She and Van are skiing in Vermont."

"How fun." Van, the dragon in question, had ended up shifting without too much help from anyone else. Seeing a real live dragon had been quite an experience. "I was wondering if I could come over and talk to you? I have some questions that I think you might be able to help me with."

"Sure, you know where the shop is. I'll be here until seven."

It was after five now. "I'll be there in about ten minutes."

"See you then."

I let Buttercup know I'd be out for a bit, then grabbed one of the company bicycles from the warehouse and rode to Willa's.

She greeted me with a warm smile and welcomed me into the back office. There was a big orange cat asleep on her desk.

I scratched his belly while she closed the door. "Who's this?"

"That's Jasper, my baby. He's such a slug. He's been there most of the day."

"How do you get any work done with him taking up your desk?"

"I don't. I have to move him, which he doesn't like. Silly beast." She tipped her head, her incredible aqua eyes sparkling. "But you didn't come here to talk about Jasper, did you?"

"No."

She nodded. "I had a feeling I'd be seeing you."

"Are you psychic? Is that a fae thing?"

She laughed. "No, but with the theft of the jewelry and there being a fae involved, I figured it was just a matter of time." Her expression grew more serious. "What can I help you with?"

"It's the fae who's involved that I want to know about. Do you know what kind he is? What powers he might have?"

"I can't tell just by looking. Our gifts don't really manifest themselves in such obvious ways. I can tell you if he's lapidus, like me. The bad news is the jewelry probably won't get returned. Not in one piece."

"What does that mean, lapidus?"

"It's the kind of fae I am. This guy most likely isn't one, though. Lapidus are pretty rare. In a nutshell, we have the ability to communicate with and control stones and metals."

"So if he was one, he probably would have taken the jewelry apart already."

She nodded. "That's what I would have done. Stripped it down to individual stones and turned the leftover metal into something else. It would make everything easier to hide and move."

"That's not good."

"Not at all. But again, lapidus are pretty rare. It wouldn't be likely that he'd be working as a DJ's assistant if he was one."

"Unless that's just his cover." Which was an interesting thought.

"True."

"What else might he be?"

She thought for a second. "I'm not sure. He could be a stone mover. That's much more common. So are abilities with air, fire, and water. Our gifts tend to be based around the elements."

I mulled this new info over. "If he had water abilities, would he be able to produce snow and ice, the way a winter elf can?"

"Not like what happened at the ball. Not with that sort of magnitude. I've never heard of it anyway."

I sighed and leaned against a filing cabinet.

She frowned. "I'm sorry I can't help you more. I left my fae life behind when I was pretty young, so it's possible that I just don't know enough to help you."

"No, you've been great. And I've taken up too much of your time already. I appreciate it. Thanks."

"Anytime. For what that's worth." She opened the office door. "Hey, how did you like the obsidian bracelet?"

"It was stunning. Unfortunately, the thief ripped it off my wrist when they took the rest of my jewelry." I pulled the safety pin from my pocket. "This is all I have left."

"Oh no, that's awful. Sinclair was so happy about that bracelet."

"So was I. You did a beautiful job with it." I started to put the pin away.

"Wait. If the thief ripped that off your wrist, that means he or she touched the bracelet. Could I see those beads again? I might be able to help after all."

"Sure." I handed her the pin.

She closed her hand around it and shut her eyes. A few seconds later, she opened them and gave the pin back to me. "The contact was brief so the impression left behind wasn't much. But there's a lot of darkness there. And duplicity."

"Lies?"

"Yes, but more than that. I don't know how else to describe what I felt as duplicity. Does that help at all?"

"It confirms what I was thinking, so yes. Thank you."

"You're welcome."

I left and got on my bike to ride back to the shop, then stopped, wondering if I should go by the sheriff's department instead. I wanted to, but then, I also knew that if Juniper was still there, I might go all rabid yeti on them. Probably better if that didn't happen. I glanced up at the darkening sky and wondered how much longer they could possibly keep her. All night? I hoped not.

Birdie had said she'd call with any news, but I wasn't sure she was even still working. Maybe she was because of everything going on. I checked my phone. I hadn't missed any messages.

Reluctantly, I rode back to the shop. I did have a business to run, after all. And not feeling like working wasn't a valid excuse. Not when you were the boss.

As I approached the warehouse, I slowed down and hopped off the bike so I could get my key out. Behind me, a car parked at the curb.

I stuck my key in the lock. The light over the door was out. I made a mental note to add that to the list of things to do.

"Jayne Frost?"

"Yes?" I turned, and with a sharp crack, everything went dark.

The back of my head throbbed with pain. I reached up to feel the spot that hurt the most, and both my hands moved together. It took half a second, but I realized they were duct-taped together. So were my feet. I blinked a few times, trying to clear my vision, but there wasn't much to see except for some shapes and outlines, and they were faintly doubled. I guess from the blow to my head.

I groaned softly, but the sound went nowhere. What was going on? Something was covering my mouth. More duct tape? It was forcing me to breathe through my nose, and the smells assaulted me. A vague oily scent. Another that was sharp, like gasoline or turpentine. More that were like cleaners and chemicals. Sort of like plastic. The ground under my cheek was hard and roughly fuzzed. Carpet. But not nice carpet. Industrial.

The space was noisy too. And it was moving.

I blinked again, trying to focus. A little red light leaked in at both ends of the enclosure. Everything shifted suddenly, causing me to roll forward. In that moment, everything made sense.

I was in a trunk. Son of a nutcracker.

I brought my hands close to my face for a better look at my restraints. There was a lot of duct tape around my wrists. I felt around my mouth. Definitely duct tape. I tried again to move my legs and felt the pressure of the tape wrapped around my ankles and just below my knees. Then I gently rolled my head back and forth. The lump on my cranium was the size of a small snowball, and I had another sore spot on the side of my neck.

The anger I'd been marinating in, the anger that had started to dissipate after seeing Willa, was back. In force.

I was not going to be held captive. No freaking way. This nonsense was coming to an end right now. I stretched my fingers out to produce a short blade I could use to cut through the duct tape.

Nothing happened.

How was that possible? I tried again. Not even a single snowflake appeared.

I'd been hit on the head, I knew that much. But had the injury caused greater damage than just the lump I could feel? Could that even happen to a winter elf?

I had no idea, but clearly something was going on. Using my fingernails, I picked at the tape over my mouth to lift one of the edges and slowly peel it off. At last I was able to take a decent breath. I tried chewing through the tape on my wrists, but there was a lot of it, and the jaw movement made my head scream in pain.

As my eyes adjusted to what little light there was, I looked around the trunk for anything I might use as a tool or a weapon. My purse was still slung across my body, but it had shifted behind me, and there was no way I could reach it with my hands taped in front of me. The trunk was empty and remarkably clean. Like it didn't get used much. I inhaled again and recognized the chemical smell I'd picked up on earlier. It was *new car*. Or newly cleaned car. Could this be a rental?

I thought about the sedan that had pulled up behind me when I was getting my key out. Something about it felt familiar, but what? I'd paid so little attention to it that trying to recall what it looked like now only made my head hurt worse. The voice I'd heard had been male. I was pretty sure about that.

If I couldn't use my ice magic, there had to be another way. I thought about using the Santa Slide. It would work, but my head already hurt from the bump. What if the dizziness made me black out and I came to in the middle of a road? I could get run over. At the very least, I'd suffer a horrifying case of road rash. Possibly break something. Which, okay, I'd recover from that, but getting run over? Not so much.

Maybe I could kick the taillights out and get help that way. I'd seen it done in movies. I positioned my feet as close to one of the red lights as I could, then kicked.

With that much duct tape restricting my movements, the kick was more like a sad bunny hop.

I tried to pull my wrists apart. The duct tape strained, but held fast. Time to suck it up and try to gnaw through it again. Whoever had tied me up understood I was stronger than an average human. Which meant they knew what I was. And probably who I was—the Winter Princess.

A flood of questions filled my head. Was this a kidnapping? Would they be asking my parents for a ransom? No, that was too coincidental. This had to be related to the diamond heist. But how? How did kidnapping me fit into that?

Maybe they were going to hold me hostage in exchange for safe passage out of town. Did that mean I was getting too close to the truth of what was going on?

The car slowed and turned, rolling me to the side. The pavement changed from smooth to rough. We were off the highway. Maybe at our final destination. Sure enough, the brake lights came on and the car stopped.

I braced myself for whatever was about to happen, and a new thought popped into my head. Was I about to die? I hoped not. Who would want me dead? I couldn't really think of anyone.

The trunk opened, and a dark, male shape was outlined by the backlight of a neon sign and a street lamp, making it impossible to see who the guy was. The roof line of a long building framed the rest of my view, allowing only a narrow sliver of night sky to peek through between it and the trunk edge.

With a grunt, he grabbed the tape I'd peeled off and slapped it back over my mouth. That brought him close enough for me to see who my captor was.

"You have got to be kidding me," I mumbled through the tape.

But Lance wasn't interested in conversation. He picked me up like a baby. The air around us blurred, and the next second, we were in a cheap motel room and my head was screaming again. What kind of magic was that? He could teleport? I had no idea fae could do that.

Then I realized why my head hurt so badly again. He hadn't teleported. He'd *carried* me in. But at a speed quicker than a human—or elf—eye could follow. That's why the air had blurred.

I wasn't sure vampires could even move like that, so finding out a fae could was even more surprising. No wonder Lance had been able to strip off everyone's jewels so quickly at the ball. But that didn't explain how he had no mark.

He tossed me on a bed, and I landed facing the back wall. He went back out to the car at normal speed. I wriggled onto my back as best I could and took the opportunity to get a better look at my surroundings. It was a cheap motel all right. The Pinehurst Inn if I had to make a bet. But then I had no idea how long I'd been in the car either. We could be in another state for all I knew.

A moan broke the silence. I wriggled around some more so I could look in that direction. There was a second bed, with a second equally tacky floral quilt. Someone was lying on it, turned away from me and curled in a semi-fetal position.

What little skin I could see was pale and clammy looking. Chalky.

I went still. Where had I seen chalky skin before? The ache in my head wouldn't let me remember.

My gaze went past the figure on the bed to the small table near the windows. There was a crumpled food bag on it. I recognized the red logo. Mrs. D's Dairy Barn.

A weird, panicky feeling snapped through me. Christmas on a cracker. The Dairy Barn. And chalky skin. They meant something. But what? *Think*. Why did those things matter? And why did I feel like I was on the verge of a panic attack? My heart was pounding, making it harder for me to breathe with the duct tape. I had to calm down, had to get a handle on what was happening. If only my head didn't hurt so much.

I was about to yank the duct tape off again when Lance came back in with a small duffel bag. He shut the door and locked it, then slumped down in a chair at the table and leaned forward like he was trying to catch his breath. He dropped the duffel bag, paying no attention to me. He wasn't looking so hot. Nearly as pale as the guy on the bed. Finally, he lifted his head and spoke to the guy.

"I've got her. We're going to get you fixed up, then we're getting out of here."

More moaning answered him.

I stared at the person on the bed. He was in street clothes like he'd just walked in and lain down. A dark hoodie and dark jeans. Shoes still on.

Fancy European sneakers.

My pulse went into overdrive. The person on the bed was the third man. The guy who'd been in the rental apartment. The guy who'd set Lark up.

I didn't think I could get angrier. I was wrong.

Lance was trying to roll the guy over and prop him up with pillows, but the guy kept sagging down. Finally, he got the man situated and came over to me.

He yanked me upright, enabling me to see the other man's face for the first time.

The Dairy Barn bag made sense now. No wonder I thought I'd seen Lance there. The man on the other bed was his twin. No goatee and shorter dark hair, but the man was Lance's double. Had the guy at the Dairy Barn been in dark jeans and those sneakers? I'd been so fixated on his face, I hadn't paid attention.

Lance ripped the tape off my mouth. "You did this to him. Now you're going to fix him, you understand?"

"No, I don't. Did what to who?"

"Don't play dumb with me. I've had enough of that from Lark."

I glared at him and spoke more slowly. "I have no idea what you are talking about."

He leaned in, his face just inches from mine. "Somehow, you hurt my brother. Infected him with frostbite. And now it's making him sick. Both of us, actually, but I'm not nearly as bad as he is. So fix him, or I will kill you. Does that help?"

I swallowed at the seriousness of the threat, but I was not about to back down. "I didn't do anything to him. I didn't even know you had a brother."

"Oh really?" He walked over to his brother and lifted his shirt. A festering black slash crossed his ribs.

"The death mark," I whispered.

"I knew you'd recognize your handiwork." He dropped the shirt back down. "You're going to remove that frostbite and make Roddy better, and there's not going to be any funny business." He pulled a gun from behind his back and pointed it at me. "Understand?"

Oh boy. "I understand you're crazy. I swear I didn't do that to him. How could I?"

"Don't play dumb. You did it at the ball."

The pounding in my head wasn't letting up, and that wasn't helping my mood, but I knew that my only hope right now was to keep him talking. "So he's the one who went through the crowd, stealing everything?"

"Look at you, figuring things out." Lance's lip curled in anger. "Fix him."

"How do you move so fast?"

Lance's hand began to shake. "Fix him, or I will shoot you."

I lifted my hands. "I can't. My magic's not working."

He lowered the gun a little. "I only gave you a small injection of saline. Your magic should be fine now. Try it."

"You injected me?" That explained the sore spot on my neck and why my magic was unusable. But how did he know the effects of salt water on winter elves? From Lark? Why would she share that kind of information?

"Just enough to keep your magic contained until we got here."

"I'd like to roll you in cheap syrup and throw you to a pack of hungry yetis." Yetis didn't eat people, but he didn't know that.

He brandished the gun again. "Fix my brother."

I wiggled my fingers. "No magic."

Lanced walked closer to me. "Try."

I made a show of trying, but I wasn't really doing anything but narrowing my eyes and thrusting my hands into the air. "See? Nothing."

He grunted. "Another couple of minutes." He went back to the table and sat in the chair, resting his arm on the table so that the gun stayed pointed at me.

I wasn't going to be able to keep up the pretense all night. Hopefully, someone would find the bike by the warehouse door, realize I was gone, and figure out where I was. I sighed. That was a lot that needed to happen.

Snowballs. This really might be my last night alive. That made me a little teary, especially when I thought about Spider and how much I was going to miss him. Maybe Sinclair would take him in. At least then Spider would have Sugar to keep him company. Would Sinclair miss me? I thought he would. I'd miss him. And Greyson and Cooper.

And my parents and my aunt and uncle, and Juniper, who had better not still be in the sheriff's office, and Buttercup and—

"Try again."

"Why should I? You're going to kill me either way, aren't you?"

A muscle in his jaw twitched. "Fix my brother and I'll let you live. Don't fix him and I'll kill you and your cat. Should I go get him? I left the carrier in the backseat of the car."

Every inch of me went cold with rage and fear. The thought of Spider being in danger made me see red. My knuckles cracked from how hard I was squeezing my hands into fists. The rush of emotion almost blinded me with frost.

Lance started laughing. "I thought that would do it."

Snowflakes drifted from the ceiling. My magic was back.

And there was no more hiding it.

Logic told me I should be calm and rational and work out a plan. But my gut wanted to put an ice dagger into Lance's heart. I could too, if I knew for sure my magic was totally back and completely stable. After whatever he'd dosed me with, I couldn't be sure. I'd seen the effects of salt water on winter elves before. And I wasn't going to risk my life—or Spider's—on an assumption.

For now, I would play along. "Clearly, I have no choice but to do as you tell me. But here's the thing. I didn't do that to your brother."

"Stop lying. That's frostbite. I've seen it before. I'm not an idiot."

That was debatable.

"It's not frostbite." Could I tell him it was the death mark of a necromancer? I'd promised to keep Sinclair's secret, but this was an extenuating circumstance. "Or maybe it is, but it's not from me.

My magic doesn't work that way." Actually, it might, in theory. I'd never tried to give someone frostbite, but that didn't mean my magic wasn't capable.

Lance gave me a strange look. "Who else would it be from? He said it happened after taking your jewelry."

"Beats me."

Lance's gaze tapered down like he was thinking. Some long seconds passed before he spoke again. "I'm going to get your cat. Then we'll see what you know."

"*No.*" I strained forward. I would kill him if he hurt Spider. "I'll help. I know how to fix it."

His lip curled like he'd known all along I'd been lying to him. "Do it, now."

"I have to be next to him and I need my hands free and I'm going to have to make an ice blade."

He snorted. "Sure, you having a weapon sounds exactly like the way to help him."

"The mark has to be cut out. It's the only way."

He glanced at his brother. "Roddy, what do you think?"

Roddy's eyes flickered open to half-mast. He looked at me and slowly shook his head. "She did this to me. She wants to kill me."

"No, I don't. All you did was steal from me, my family, and friends. And set my ex-best friend up to take the fall. So while I hate you because you're scummy garbage with the morals of a yeti in heat, I don't want to see you dead. I would much rather prefer that you rot in jail, and for that, you maggot-brained lump of yellow snow, you need to be alive."

Lance jerked the gun up higher. His whole body was shaking. "You think a lot of yourself, don't you, Princess?"

"I think if you hurt me or my cat, then I'll change my opinion on whether or not you ought to be dead."

The temperature in the room dropped sharply. I hadn't done it either. Then the door rattled like a sharp wind had blown past, and a ghostly figure appeared in the room.

What in the name of Christmas was going on?

An old woman in a long flannel nightgown and a sleeping cap floated toward me. I could see right through her. Awesome. I'd been wondering when the hallucinations were going to kick in.

She pointed a finger at me. "Jayne Frost."

"Yes, ma'am." There was no reason not to be polite. She didn't look threatening. And I could use a friend.

"You okay?"

"I've been better. I've got a lump on my head, I've been drugged, and there's a lot of duct tape on me, but other than that, I'm hanging in there."

"Good girl." Then she looked at Lance and his

brother. Both of them were staring at the woman with wide eyes. She pointed at them. "Twins?"

They both nodded.

"Quicksilver fae," she muttered.

They nodded again.

She clucked her tongue in that disapproving way old women had. "That explains a lot." Then she pointed at me. "Sit tight."

The door rattled again, and she disappeared in a whoosh of wind.

"What was that?" Lance raised his voice and looked at me, punctuating his words with the gun. "Did you do that? Was that some frost ghost?"

"Frost ghosts aren't even a thing. Frost giants, now—"

The window shattered, sending glass everywhere as a man came flying through it. I recognized the silver streaks immediately.

"Sinclair!"

He landed on his feet, shook the glass shards off, and launched at Lance, fist first. Lance backed up, but there was no escaping Sinclair's punch. Lance's gun went off, filling the room with a flash of light and an explosion of noise. I cringed as smoke curled through the air along with an acrid smell, but neither Lance nor Sinclair stopped fighting.

Roddy was reaching for his brother. I had no idea what he was up to, but I wasn't waiting to find out.

I lifted my hands and used my magic to freeze Roddy in place on the bed, then made an ice blade and started sawing at the duct tape on my legs and ankles.

Two punches later, Sinclair had knocked Lance out cold. The fae collapsed crossways over his frozen brother on the bed.

Sinclair stepped back, chest heaving with the exertion. His knuckles were bruised and bloody. I wasn't sure if that was from Lance's lip or his own injuries. "You'd better freeze him too."

I turned Lance into a matching slab of ice like his brother, then held the blade out to Sinclair. "I can't do the tape around my wrists."

He leaped over the bed to where I was and took the blade. "You okay?"

"Yes. How did you find me?"

"Long story. Willa helped. And Ada did the recon."

"Ada?"

"The ghost."

"Oh." I was guessing Ada was a big part of that long story. "Is that another necromancer thing?"

"Yes. Do you want me to explain now?"

"No. That can wait."

"I'm so glad you're okay." He smiled and kissed my head.

"Me too. Thanks for finding me."

"Willa made that happen. You should thank

her." He looked over his shoulder at the broken window. Willa was standing on the other side. She waved at me, then pointed to the phone pressed to her ear. "Sheriff," she mouthed.

I nodded since Sinclair wasn't quite done freeing me. He was going slowly, probably because the ice blade was sharp, the duct tape tight, and he didn't want to risk nicking me.

"Almost done," he said.

I looked up at him. He leaned down and kissed me again, like he couldn't stop himself. It was just a short, quick one, then he straightened and went back to work. "I was so worried about you. If they had hurt you…"

His voice trailed off in a growl of anger, and his eyes gleamed with a light I'd never seen before.

"I'm so glad you two figured things out." I leaned my throbbing head on his shoulder. The leather was oddly rough. "They have Spider. He's in a carrier in the car."

"We'll get him out."

The roughness of the leather irritated my already hurting head. I moved back to inspect the strange texture. There was a hole in the shoulder of his jacket. I stared at it while he finished unwrapping the duct tape from my wrists. The shirt beneath the leather looked wet.

"Son of a nutcracker," I whispered as a new chill took hold of me. "You got shot."

"I'm okay." He peeled the last strip of duct tape off.

I stood up and pulled the jacket away from his body. His black T-shirt clung to him, soaked through with blood. I gasped and my head went wobbly. Then my knees. I fought the instinct to pass out.

"Willa." My voice sounded so weak for someone who was yelling. Was I yelling? I was trying to yell, that much I knew. "Call an ambulance. Sinclair's been shot. And get Spider out of the car. Make sure my baby is okay."

Then darkness closed in, and I passed out for the second time that evening.

I came to in a much more comfortable position than I had the first time. Mostly because I was on a stretcher. My head still hurt like there was a yeti gnawing on it, but at least I wasn't restrained. I tried to sit up and couldn't. Okay, so I was restrained. Straps ran across my chest and legs. "Why am I tied down? I need to see my cat. And my boyfriend. And Willa."

"Don't move, Miss Frost. You've got a concussion." The paramedic shined a penlight in my eyes.

"Great, good to know. Where is my cat? Is Spider okay? He's in the car in front of the hotel room. Where's Sinclair? Willa!"

"I'm here, Jayne." A hand covered mine.

I squinted against the light. I could just make out Willa's halo of honey-blond hair. And behind her, more lights flashing red and blue like carnival rides. "Where's Sinclair? Is he okay? Did you get Spider out of the car? Lance said he had him in a carrier. He was going to k-k-kill him." I burst into tears.

Willa patted my hand. "Sinclair is on his way to the hospital in a different ambulance. He should be just fine. Lance and his brother are on their way to jail, where they will be defrosted. As for Spider, there was no carrier or cat in the car. I'm sure they were bluffing. I can have someone check, though. Who has access to your apartment?"

"Miss Frost, we need to transport you to the hospital now."

I glanced up at the paramedic. He was an older man with a kindly face and the eyes of a wolf. I liked him. "Can Willa come with me?"

"Sure."

Willa climbed aboard as they closed the ambulance doors, still holding my hand.

I squeezed her hand and thought about her question. Who had access to my apartment? "Can you call Juniper and ask her if—Juniper!" I tried to sit up again. "She better not still be at the sheriff's department."

The ambulance's windows frosted over, and a few flakes drifted down.

"Miss Frost." The paramedic's warm hand settled on my shoulder. "I need you to stay calm. Everything is being handled."

Willa smiled at me. She was so pretty. "I can find out, okay? Nick, my boyfriend, he fills in as a part-time deputy."

"Okay," I whispered. My head was still killing me. I needed something else to focus on. I patted the pocket of my jeans until I found what I was looking for. The safety pin with the beads on it. I dug it out and worried the beads. Touching them made me feel better.

Willa dialed. "Hi, honey. I need you to do something for me. Can you call the station and check on the status of Juniper…" She looked at me.

"Trembley," I supplied.

"Juniper Trembley. Yes. Thanks." She hung up. "He's going to text me. What else can I do for you?"

The frost disappeared. "How did you help Sinclair find me?"

"Those obsidian beads in your hand. Since I touched them, I knew their signature. And because I made the bracelet and I still had a few of the original strand left over, I was able to use those beads to call for the ones you were carrying."

I thought about that, and despite the pain, something pretty obvious occurred to me. "You touched the Heart of Dawn. You could find that too, then, right?"

She shook her head. "Sadly, no. I'd have to have a piece of the rough, the original stone the diamond was cut from. If I had that, I could. But stone calls to stone. I just know how to listen."

"Oh."

Willa glanced down at her phone. "Nick says Juniper hasn't been at the station for hours."

"That's good."

"How about I text her and ask her to check on Spider?"

"Her number is in my phone. Which is in my purse. Which is who knows where?"

The paramedic patted something at my side. "Your bag is right here."

Willa picked it up. "I'll take care of getting ahold of Juniper."

"Thanks." Knowing Spider was okay would be a big weight off of me, but this mess wasn't going to be truly over until the jewelry was found and I knew Sinclair was okay. The man had taken a bullet rescuing me.

I stared up at the ambulance's roof. A bullet. That was kind of amazing. And based on the blood I'd seen, necromancers didn't look particularly fast-healing or even slightly immortal.

He could have died.

The man I was absolutely, unquestionably, terrifyingly falling in love with could have died.

We really needed to talk.

Turns out Sinclair wasn't the only one who'd lost some blood. The lump on my head was more of a gaping head wound and required six staples to close it up and a tetanus shot and an overnight stay in the hospital for *observation*. Much to my displeasure. About all of it. The staples and the tetanus shot both hurt, and I wasn't thrilled about spending the night in the hospital.

I wanted to go home and see Spider, who was currently being catsat by Aunties Juniper and Buttercup. I was sure they were spoiling him with too many treats and too many bowls of Chicken Party, but I probably would be doing that too as soon as I got home. I missed his furry face and his sweet little meows and him telling me he was hungry.

I missed Sinclair's face, too. I really wanted to talk to him and tell him thank you. He'd saved my life. I have no doubt about that.

From what the nurses had told me, he'd needed surgery to remove the bullet. I'd almost cried again hearing that. To think he'd had a bullet in him and had only been concerned with cutting me free from that duct tape. Maybe it had been adrenaline keeping him from feeling the pain. Or maybe he was just that stubborn.

Or maybe—and this was a big one—he was a little bit in love with me too.

Birdie was my first visitor the next morning. I'm pretty sure she snuck in before visiting hours actually started, because there wasn't much light filtering through the slats of the window blinds. Also, she was whispering when she came in.

"Princess," she hissed. "You awake?"

I hadn't been. Not fully. "Hmm? Yes," I mumbled.

"Good." She came over to the bed. "How are you?"

I thought about that a second. I had a dull headache, but otherwise didn't feel too bad. Weak, but a quick glance at the IV in my arm explained that. Saline. Salt water was a winter elf's kryptonite, and I'd already had a small dose from Lance. The good news was it generally wore off pretty quickly when given in small batches. "I'm pretty good, considering."

"That's great news." Her smile bent into something a little less happy and a lot more apologetic. "I'm really sorry I couldn't help you with this investigation more. I was stuck between a rock and a hard spot here. Your father and my nephew, respectively."

"Yeah, I know. Don't feel bad for doing your job." I wasn't mad at her. Just because she'd helped me so much in the past didn't mean I could expect her to put her neck on the line for me every single time.

Her smile brightened. "Well, I do feel bad. A little. But I figured out a way to make it up to you. I think." She dug into her enormous plaid handbag and retrieved a tablet. "Hank is out processing Lark this morning. I thought you might like to see it. He's going to do one last brief interrogation with her, then she'll be released."

I wasn't 100 percent on why Birdie thought I'd want to see that, but I was sort of curious. And hey, why not? Maybe it would bring me some closure. Come to think of it, Birdie actually had made a pretty reasonable assumption. "Fire it up."

Birdie tapped a few things on the screen, then typed in a web address, and a few seconds later, a camera feed popped up.

It showed the cell where Lark was being held.

"There are cameras in there?" I didn't remember seeing them when I'd been there, but I hadn't been looking for them, either.

"Oh, sure," Birdie said, like it was a foregone

conclusion. She pointed at the screen. "There's Hank now. Lemme turn up the sound."

She pushed a button on the side, and some ambient noises filtered through.

Lark got off the bench as Hank approached. "What now? It better be to let me out. I'm not just anyone, you know. I'm the Ice Queen. I have shows to do. If I don't turn up for those, people will be looking for me."

Birdie sniffed. "She sure has a big feeling about herself. Ice Queen. Hmph."

"Agreed." I guess that was Lark's way of being royalty after all.

Hank hooked his thumbs into his utility belt, seemingly unimpressed with Lark's supposed celebrity. "We found your boyfriend."

She straightened. "And?"

"He was holed up at the Pinehurst Inn. Tried to kill your friend Jayne."

"Are you serious?" She mumbled something under her breath.

I put my hand on Birdie's arm and leaned closer to the screen. "What did she say?"

"Not sure."

"Can you go back? Turn up the sound?"

"I can try, hang on." Birdie fiddled with something. The video sped backward, then started playing again.

"Are you serious?" Lark muttered, "Those idiots."

"Sweet fancy Christmas." I squeezed Birdie's arm. "Birdie."

She hit pause. "What is it, Princess?"

"Lark knew." I felt the rush of urgency. "Call Hank. He can't release her."

"Lark knew what, honey?"

I stared at her. "Lark said *those idiots*. Plural. Not singular. If she didn't know about Lance's twin, wouldn't she have said *that idiot*?"

"Butter my biscuit. You're right."

"Unless Sheriff Merrow already told her Lance has a twin?"

"You saw him come in. That's the first he's talked to her since leaving the Pinehurst Inn."

Suddenly, it all came together. "They didn't find the jewelry at the motel, did they?"

"Nope, they didn't. I'm sorry."

"Don't be. I know where it is." I gave her a sly look. "You in?"

"I'm as in as you can get."

I whipped the covers back. "Let's ditch this joint."

"You sure you're up to that?"

I nodded. "My blood sugar might be a little low and my magic is going to be on the fritz for a bit, but I can manage. Are my clothes here?"

"On the chair in that bag. I should have brought you some clean ones. I didn't know you were going to break out."

"I can manage in dirty clothes. What we're going to do isn't going to take long."

While Birdie called Hank, I eased the IV out, then got dressed. My strength would come back soon enough, but for now I'd pass it off as part of being whacked on the head. Birdie played lookout, and once the coast was clear, we snuck out. Actually, we walked out. It was early and no one paid that much attention to us.

I thought about trying to find Sinclair first, but as much as I wanted to see him, I knew Lark had to be dealt with.

Birdie drove, and fifteen minutes later (and minus one chocolate chip granola bar, which Birdie kept a supply of in her handbag), we were climbing the stairs to Lark and Lance's rental apartment.

Birdie followed me. "Are you sure you're okay? One granola bar isn't going to give you much energy."

I was hungry, a little weak, temporarily out of magic, and wearing yesterday's clothes that may or may not have had a few bloodstains on them, but nothing was going to stop me now. "We can eat after this is handled."

"Doughnuts?"

I didn't need to see her face to know she was smiling. "Sinclair's still in the hospital. I'm not sure there's going to be any doughnuts today."

"Oh. Right." She sighed. "You want to go back and see him after this?"

"Yes. But I might shower first. And check on Spider. Besides, visiting hours don't actually start for another hour or two yet. There's time."

We got to the apartment door. I pushed a little magic into my fingers to see how things were going. My fingertips frosted over. Lightly. It would have to do. I turned to face Birdie. She'd seen me do the Santa Slide before. "Okay, this is going to take a little extra time. I may even pass out when I get through, but don't freak. I'll come around. This magic is just draining, and I'm already not at peak level."

She frowned. "I could just break the door down."

"Um, isn't this technically a crime scene? Doesn't everything need to be intact? I mean, for official purposes?"

"It does," a gravelly voice from the stairwell answered. Sheriff Merrow was coming toward us.

Birdie clapped. "Hank, honey, you came."

I gave her a look. "You called him?"

She raised her brows. "I did."

He joined us on the landing, his gaze settling on me. "Aren't you supposed to be in the hospital?"

"Sure, but this is more important. And I'm fine. Are you going to tell my father about this?"

"Depends on what we find in here." He snorted and produced a key. "I'll open the door."

"Thank you." I was all about not passing out.

He got us in, then shut the door behind us. "All right, where's this jewelry? We've searched every inch of this place."

There was no doubt they had, but something told me they'd overlooked one spot. And that's exactly what Lark had been counting on. "I'm about to show you."

I walked into the kitchen and went through the drawers until I found a big knife. Without my magic at full strength, this would have to do.

Birdie's brows shot up. "You really need that?"

I yanked open the freezer. It was still clogged with ice. "I do if I'm going to get through this."

Two rather ineffective whacks with the blade and Sheriff Merrow came over. "Let me."

He took his nightstick off his belt and cracked the ice with one hard blow. A huge frosty chunk fell onto the kitchen floor, revealing a fabric-wrapped bundle. "How about that?"

He took the bundle out and unwrapped it.

The Heart of Dawn was front and center. He shook his head as he looked at me. "I don't know how you figured this out, but I'm glad you did."

"Way to go, Princess," Birdie exclaimed.

Sheriff Merrow squeezed the radio at his shoulder. "Deputy Blythe, be informed that I am returning to the station with evidence. Further interrogation of the suspect to follow."

"Roger that," she answered. "You want Cruz and me to meet you there?"

"Roger." He clicked off and looked at me. "Are Lark's prints going to be on this?"

"Unless she wore gloves. I think you'll find Roddy's too. I'm not sure about Lance's. I don't think he ever touched it. But I do know neither he nor his brother had any idea the jewelry was here."

He wrapped the bundle back up. "Tell me how you got to this point."

I hopped up onto the counter to sit. "Lark and Lance had what? Forty-five minutes between leaving the ball and you guys taking them into custody?"

"Give or take."

"I don't think she was ever drugged or tired or anything like that. I think the twins *tried* to drug her to make her shimmer go haywire, but she figured it out a year ago when they made their first attempt and played along so they'd believe she was an easy mark."

The sheriff nodded. "That was the first time she said her shimmer went wrong."

"Yep," I continued. "That's when she figured out what they were up to and who they really were. And how she was going to use their greed for her own purposes."

Birdie made a throaty, disgusted noise. "She's the greedy one."

"No argument there," I said. Even in college she'd wanted what wasn't hers. "So she set the twins up, letting them think she would be an easy pawn. I don't know how she knew they were thieves. I'm guessing these two have a long history of heists."

"We did uncover a string of robberies that took place in Europe. Each one in the same city she was performing in."

Birdie rolled her eyes. "There you go."

"Except," the sheriff said, "there was no other evidence it was the twins. The best any security camera footage could make out was a blur. Even slowed down it was a blur."

Birdie nodded. "Just like in the footage I pulled from the security cameras at that bed and breakfast that got robbed. We thought it was a moth shifter."

The sheriff's brows lifted. "You thought it was a moth shifter." He looked at me again. "Go on."

"Lark must have known they were quicksilver fae. She's traveled a lot and met all kinds of people. Her experiences have probably taught her all sorts of things."

The sheriff crossed his arms. "So she sets them up, knowing she's got this gig at Elenora's and what a score that's going to be."

"Right. And from the DJ booth, she could see everything that was going on. She saw Roddy take the jewelry. Saw him stumble as he went by me and Sinclair. Probably didn't understand what had happened, but knew something had gone a little off script."

The sheriff squinted like he could see the scene play out. "But he still left with the jewelry."

"Yes. And Lark saw all that too," I continued. "As soon as Lark and Lance left Elenora's, they came back here. She faked an argument. Something to get worked up about, enough that she could use her anger as an excuse to freeze him. Then she went to the Pinehurst Inn, froze Roddy, took the jewelry, and came back here where she squirreled it all away in the freezer, hidden behind the ice. I'm guessing the bulk of the frost was already there. Or that she'd been building it up since they first arrived so that Lance would think it had been like that. What she didn't plan on was Lance planting those loose diamonds to make it seem like the stolen jewels were in the DJ booth. Then the rest played out like we all saw."

"Sounds plausible," Sheriff Merrow said. "Especially with what we've uncovered on our end."

I sighed. I wish he'd share his info. "The only thing I can't figure is how she knew where Roddy was staying."

"I can answer that." He narrowed his eyes. "We found a second phone in the lining of her purse. It's a clone of Lance's phone. She was getting all his messages. She could have even been listening in on his calls."

"For real?" I asked. "You can do that?"

Birdie shrugged. "It's easy. You just copy the sim card."

Sheriff Merrow gave his aunt the side eye. "It's scary how much you know sometimes."

She grinned. "Isn't it, though?"

I pushed my hair out of my face. "I fully believe Lark's been planning this since she got the DJ job. And she's been setting the twins up about that long too. Unbelievable. But actually totally believable, given her talent for deception. She's just that devious. She even did a test run of her magic going haywire to make it seem like there was a precedent."

"This is plenty for me to go on." The sheriff shifted like he was ready to go. "I'll get it all out of her."

"If you need a little help, threaten her with salt water."

His brows lifted in question.

"Winter elves don't like to talk about it much, but salt water strips away our magic like, well, magic. It's why I didn't have the strength to chip through that ice. I had an IV at the hospital."

Birdie sucked in a breath. "Saline."

"Yep. But let's keep that a secret between us, okay?"

The sheriff smiled. "After finding this jewelry, you can have all the secrets you want."

My phone rang. Took me a couple seconds to shake off the sleep enough to realize that's what the sound was. I felt around on my nightstand until my hand connected with it. I managed to tap the right spot on the screen to answer. "Hello," I mumbled.

"Sorry to wake you, Miss Frost. Just wanted to give you an update, but that can wait." Sheriff Merrow's voice was low and comforting. "Call me back when you're up to it."

"No, I'm good." I rolled over and pushed myself upright. I was a little stiff, and I had no clue what time it was. Or day, for that matter. But my head felt pretty good. That was something. "What's the news?"

"Lark confessed to everything. It went down pretty much the way you suspected. Too hard to deny when faced with the evidence of her crime."

I nodded. Like he could see me. "Were her fingerprints on the jewelry?"

"Yes. And Roddy's."

Spider was sprawled on the second pillow looking about as cute as I could stand. "What's going to happen to them?"

"Lark pleaded for mercy, but I'm not in a position to offer that. She'll be transported back to the North Pole for trial and sentencing."

"Elenora approved that?"

"She got her diamond back, and her guests' jewelry has all been recovered, including all of your family's pieces, so she's essentially signed off on the whole thing. Plus, she agrees that what remains is winter elf business."

"True."

I had a feeling about what my father would do to Lark. Permanently strip her of her magic (more salt water but in a much more intensive way) and ban her from the North Pole. The latter wouldn't bother Lark. She hadn't been back to the NP in years. But stripping away her magic would cost her. Hard to be the Ice Queen when you couldn't make ice.

I wasn't going to feel sorry for her. I almost died because of her. "What about Roddy and Lance?"

"Through their fingerprints, we were able to match them to that string of heists in Europe, and the petty thefts here. As soon as Roddy is released from medical care, he and his brother will be picked up by Interpol."

"Wow."

"Uh huh. Quite a catch for the Nocturne Falls Sheriff's Department." He laughed softly. "Sorry about telling you to stay out of it."

"You were just doing what my father asked."

"You knew about that?"

"I did."

"Birdie?"

I scratched Spider's head. "No comment."

He laughed again. "Sounds about right. You take care of yourself, Miss Frost. Call if you need anything."

"Thank you, Sheriff." I hung up and lay back down, my phone on my chest. A second later I picked it back up to check the day and time. I'd been out for nearly ten hours.

I felt better, so I must have needed it.

But I was starving. And I hadn't talked to Sinclair yet. I squinted up at the ceiling. I think my plan had been to come home after finding the jewelry, lie down on the couch for a little bit, then go see him. So much for a little bit. Also, how had I ended up in bed? I must have sleepwalked.

I called him. I needed to hear his voice, but I'd settle for voice mail. Happily, he answered.

"Hello, sleepy head."

I grinned. "How did you know I was sleeping?"

"Birdie came to see me, told me she'd stopped by to see you first and you were passed out."

I wonder if that's who put me in bed? She did have a key. "Are you home now? Or still in the hospital?"

"Home."

"How are you doing?"

"Sore, but I'll live. My arm will be in a sling for a while, which is going to make work tough, but I'll manage. More importantly, how are you doing?"

"I'm fine. Especially because you saved my life." My throat clogged with emotion. "Sinclair, I don't know how to say thank you enough. I owe you." Although, I was starting to get an idea of how to pay him back.

He laughed. "I don't think I saved your life."

"You did. And that's the end of that discussion. When can I see you? Because I really need to see you."

He sighed longingly. "I really need to see you too. You want to come over and have pizza?"

"That is exactly what I want to do. But I need to shower and check in on the shop."

"How about seven? That'll give you two hours. Enough time?"

"Perfect. See you then."

I got out of bed, sitting on the edge for just a second to let myself adjust to being upright.

Spider jumped down and sat by my feet.

He gazed up at me, eyes wide. "Mama sick?"

"Not anymore, baby. I feel much better now."

"Spider loves Mama."

"I love you too."

He stood up, tail high in the air. "Spider loves Chicken Party."

I smiled. "I bet you could go for some right now, too, huh? Let's go get you some dinner."

I fed him, then got into the shower. The hot water felt amazing, but I didn't linger. I had too much to do. Jeans, a cute top, and a cardigan were about the dressiest I could manage, but I doubted anyone would care. I dried my hair carefully avoiding the staples, added a little makeup, then threw my keys and my phone into my purse and went down to the shop. I figured I'd check in with Buttercup, call my dad from my office, then head over to Sinclair's.

The shop was busy, but Buttercup broke away from the register to give me a big hug. She wasn't normally a hugger, being all gamer-Goth girl that she was, so I didn't hold on to her for too long. "How are you doing?"

"I'm good. I owe you and Juniper for taking care of Spider. And this place."

"Nah. That's what friends—and employees—are for."

"Well, I appreciate it very much. How's Juni doing after being interrogated?"

Buttercup's grin held pride. "She's doing great. She's stronger than you think."

"I'm glad to hear that, but I still feel bad it happened."

Buttercup shrugged. "She'll tell you herself that it wasn't your fault."

"I guess. Anything I need to know about?"

She tipped her head like she was thinking. "We could use another shipment of Pocket Pets. Otherwise, we're golden. Things are good."

"Okay, I'm going to call my dad now anyway. I'll tell him. Then I'm going over to see Sinclair."

She grinned. "Cool. I dig him."

"I know. You like him because he's a necromancer."

She slanted her eyes at me. "You like him because he makes doughnuts."

The bells over the door chimed as a customer came in. I was about to tell Buttercup that I'd let her get back to work when I saw who the customer was.

"Hi, Greyson."

"Hey, beautiful." He held out the enormous bunch of flowers he was carrying. "I was going to leave these for you, but I'm happier to give them to you in person. How are you?"

"I'm great." I took the flowers. "And these are gorgeous."

"Do you have a second to talk, or are you swamped?"

"I can spare a minute. C'mon back to the break room. There's vase in there."

He followed me into the warehouse. "The sheriff filled me in on Lark and the twins. Crazy."

I nodded as I filled the vase from the break room sink. "Isn't it?"

He was silent while I arranged the flowers, and when I turned around, I could tell there was something on his mind. "What's up?"

He sighed and leaned against the other counter. "It's not really my business, but I have to ask. Are you seeing Sinclair Crowe?"

"I am."

Greyson's eyes took on a serious light. "He's a necromancer."

"I know." I put the flowers on the table. I'd take them up to my apartment tomorrow.

He shoved his hand through his hair. "They're dangerous, Jayne."

"So are vampires, but he hasn't complained about you."

Greyson frowned. "They're dangerous in more ways than you know. And they are *especially* dangerous to vampires."

Was Greyson jealous? I crossed my arms and wondered how this was going to go. "How so?"

"Necromancers can bring the dead back to life."

"Temporarily. And so?"

His eyes narrowed. "Do you know what would

happen to me if Sinclair brought me back to life? Let me tell you. My age would catch up to me. In a matter of seconds. I would grow old and wither into dust."

I uncrossed my arms. "Are you sure? I'm not doubting you, but that seems kind of a severe reaction to—"

"It's how my sire died." The muscles in his jaw tensed. "I watched her crumble into dust before my eyes. It's not something I'll ever forget."

"Sinclair killed your sire?" Could his death touch do that?

"Not him, another necromancer. But I know what he's capable of."

"Sinclair isn't a killer." I had to wonder if the Ellinghams knew about this. I figured they must. They approved all the new businesses in town. And none of them had made a fuss about Sinclair coming to the ball with me. "He would never do something like that."

"You know him that well?"

I frowned right back at Greyson. "I think I'm a decent judge of character."

"Like you thought Lark deserved a second chance?"

I rolled my eyes. "He saved my life. And this isn't the same thing at all."

"It is for me. What if he suddenly decides he wants you all to himself? That I'm too much competition? One touch and I'm done. He might have saved your life, but he likes you. Ask him how he feels about vampires next time you see him."

"He wouldn't hurt you."

"Are you willing to bet my life on that?"

We stared at each other for a long moment. I had a sinking feeling I wasn't going to like the answer to the question I was about to ask. "What outcome are you hoping for here?"

Greyson straightened. "I like you a lot, Jayne. I care about you more than I've cared about anyone else in a long time. But it's him or me."

My mouth dropped open. "You're giving me an ultimatum? You've never had an issue with me dating Cooper."

"A summer elf has never killed anyone I love." He bent his head a little. "It's bad enough I have to live in the same town as Sinclair. But to share you with him? I can't, Jayne. I just can't. I'm sorry."

"I'm not going to stop seeing him." That wouldn't be fair to Sinclair. And while my heart hurt, I had no claim to Greyson. Not when I was also dating Cooper. We'd always said things were casual and had agreed to no commitments. But that didn't mean this wasn't a painful moment. I nodded, a little numb. "Are we still going to be friends?"

He moved with vampire quickness to pull me into his arms. He kissed my forehead. "I hope so.

You can always call me if you need me. I want you to know that. Or if you change your mind."

I swallowed, trying to work out what was happening. I was being dumped. And it sucked. "Thanks," I whispered.

"This doesn't mean I don't still care about you. I do. I just need distance from him."

I sighed. Saying I understood would be a lie. But I wasn't up for any further discussion about how dangerous Sinclair was. The man had saved my life. Nothing was going to make me turn my back on him now. "Take care of yourself, Greyson."

"You too, Jayne." Then he was gone, the warehouse door opening and closing a second later.

I was sort of glad he left with the speed of his kind. That way, he didn't have to see the tears I wiped away.

I composed myself enough to call my dad, bring him up to speed on everything with Lark and myself, then ask him about my special request for Sinclair. Considering the circumstances, he obliged me without the slightest hesitation. Maybe he sensed my general malaise over being dumped. Maybe he felt it was paying back a kindness. Or maybe he thought I was still recovering from the kidnapping and wanted to do something to make me happy. Either way, he did what all fathers who love their daughters do—he said yes to my request.

I hung up with him and checked the time. I had about thirty minutes before I needed to leave for Sinclair's. Enough time to get through some of the backlogged emails that were undoubtedly waiting on me.

Firing up my computer proved I was right. My inbox showed ninety-eight new messages. With a sigh and a click, I headed in.

There were three from Cooper. I opened the oldest one first and read.

Hey Jayne,

Hope all is well with you. Hope Lark is being cool. Sorry I've been so out of touch. My mom isn't progressing like any of us had hoped. It's going to be a long recovery. I should have called, I know, but I'm not feeling much like talking these days. And the hospital isn't big on cell phones.

I'm sorry. This feels like a conversation best had in person, but I'm not sure when I'll be back in Nocturne Falls. And that's really what this is about. I'm staying here. At least for the next six months. Or longer. Until my mom is on her feet again. It's too much for my dad to handle by himself.

I love you. And I think you love me too. At least a little. But I've come to realize these past couple of weeks that life is short. Even for supernaturals like us. And whatever our feelings for each other, they're not leading us down the path to forever. That sounds corny in my head even as I type it, but I don't know how else to say that we should put us on the back burner. At least for now.

We both deserve more, don't you think? Doesn't mean we can't be friends. I hope we can be. Always. And this letter isn't because I've met someone else. A relationship is the furthest thing from my mind right now. Getting my mom well is my only focus here.

I guess I've rambled enough. Call me when you're free. If you want to talk. If not, I understand that too.

Cooper

I stared at the screen as more tears welled up. Wow. What a day. I read the other two emails from him, both were the about the same, him checking to see if I was still talking to him because I hadn't called or emailed back.

I hit reply, but it took me a few minutes to process what he'd said and find my own words to answer with.

Hi Cooper,

I'm so sorry to hear about your mom. I hope her recovery improves. She's so lucky to have you. I think it's incredible that you're staying there to help. I'm not mad. About any of it. I understand. I would do the same thing if it was my mom. That willingness to help is a big part of what I've always loved about you. Because yes, I do love you. I suspect part of me always will. But you're right that we weren't immediately headed toward anything concrete, so I absolutely understand what you're saying.

I will always consider you a friend. When you get back to Nocturne Falls, please let me know. And please send me updates about your mom when you get the chance.

As for Lark, that's a whole long story, but the short version is, you were right. She didn't change. I'll fill you in when we talk next.

All the best,

Jayne

I reread the message three times, then stared at the screen for five minutes until I got the courage to hit send.

When I tapped that button, a few more tears fell. If Sinclair broke up with me, I was moving home.

I ran back up to my apartment, washed my face, fixed my makeup, kissed Spider, and then left for Sinclair's. The walk in the cool air did me good. I had time to think and process and grieve a little.

To be honest, I thought my first breakup with Cooper was going to kill me, and I'd lived through that. I'd get through losing Greyson and Cooper (again). Having Sinclair would help. A lot. And both Greyson and Cooper had valid reasons. Although Cooper's was more valid, in my opinion, whereas Greyson was being a little paranoid. But whatever. We were all adults and capable of making our own decisions.

Besides, I'd never wanted things to get too serious. And it wasn't like I was completely unwanted by every male being on the planet. Sinclair wanted me. And he was a great guy who'd come to my rescue on more than one occasion. I dug into my purse and found the safety pin with the three remaining obsidian beads on it and squeezed it in my hand.

Willa's help, those three little beads, and the man who'd given them to me, were the reasons I was still here.

By the time I reached Zombie Donuts, my pity party was over. Mostly. I was still a tiny bit blue about Cooper and Greyson. Time would help.

I rang the buzzer at the street door.

Sinclair opened it about two seconds later and greeted me with a big smile. "Hey."

"You must have been watching for me from the window."

"I was. I'm glad you're here." He leaned in and kissed me.

"I'm glad I'm here too." I glanced at his arm resting in the sling. "Are you in pain?"

"Not much." He tipped his head toward the stairs. "C'mon, pizza's in the oven keeping warm."

We settled in at the table with the pizza and a bottle of wine. Sinclair had put the fireplace channel on his television, and it snapped and crackled like the real thing. It was surprisingly comforting. Sugar was asleep on the back of the couch.

I opened the wine since that was a two-handed task.

He slid a slice onto each of our plates before sitting down. "I'm glad you came over."

"Me too."

"Rough day, huh?"

I laughed. "I'm not sure where to start." I poured two glasses and took my seat.

He closed the pizza box and took my hand, kissing my knuckles. "You don't have to talk about it unless you want to."

"Thanks." I had a bite of pizza. Greyson's words were ringing in my ears. "How do you feel about vampires?"

"Pretty much the same way I do about all supernaturals." He shrugged, then winced. "I need to remember not to do that. Anyway, vampires are just people too. You know what I mean." He sipped his wine. "Why? Did one of the Ellinghams say something?"

"No. What would they have said something about?"

He set his glass down. "Some vampires have a great fear of necromancers because of our abilities. And how those abilities can affect them specifically."

"The whole bringing them back to life which actually kills them thing?"

He nodded. "Right. Which is why I signed the agreement with the Ellinghams."

"What agreement?"

"That I would never use my powers against another citizen of Nocturne Falls so long as I live and work within town limits."

"Wow, you made that promise?" Apparently, Greyson didn't know about that. Or he knew and didn't trust it. Actually, that was more likely.

"I did."

"You must have really wanted to live in Nocturne Falls."

"What I wanted was a place where I could be myself and hopefully be accepted without judgment. This town seemed like that place. A home, you know? A place to settle."

"How has that worked out so far?"

He smiled at me. "So far, pretty good." He held up his hand. "Hang on." He got up, went somewhere in the apartment, and came back with a small box. "For you."

I opened it. Inside was a new rainbow obsidian bracelet. "Oh, I love it." I put it on immediately, impressed that he'd already had a new one made. "You know that first bracelet is what saved me."

"You carrying those beads is what saved you. It allowed Willa to find you." He glanced down at his plate. "I can't imagine what I would have done if those fae had hurt you. Broken my promise to the Ellinghams, I suppose."

"No, you wouldn't have."

He looked up. "Jayne, I don't think you understand how taken with you I am."

I smiled. "I think I do. But you said that agreement only applied to citizens of Nocturne Falls. Lark, Lance, and Roddy were visitors."

He laughed, crinkling the lines around his eyes. "True." He reached over and twirled a strand of my hair around his finger. "I am *crazy* about you, Jayne Frost. I know you're dating other guys, but I don't care. I'm going to fight for you."

"You won't have to fight too hard."

"Why's that?"

"They both dumped me today. Sort of." I held up my hands. "I don't really want to talk about it, either. They had their reasons and we're all still friends and that's that."

He was smiling, but it looked like he was trying not to. "Are you sad?"

"A little. But I can see you're not."

He laughed. "I feel like life just handed me a gift."

"Then you're really going to like this. I talked to my dad before I came over here. He's sending a baker from the North Pole kitchens down to Nocturne Falls. Archie Tingle has been a head baker for over thirty years. The man can bake anything. And he will be here for as long as you need help making doughnuts."

Sinclair stared at me so long I wasn't sure my surprise was being well received. "Are you serious?"

I nodded, still unsure. "Is that okay? I told my dad how you rescued me and how you were injured and told him we should do something to help. I promise Archie can make doughnuts. And he'll do them exactly like you say."

"Okay? It's...amazing. The fact that I'll be able to keep my business going is everything. I can't thank you enough."

"You already have. This is my thanks to you. My family's thanks, really."

"Well, we're even. I'm serious. This is so much more than I expected. Wow." He sat back and put his hand on his forehead. "I should have gotten you a bigger bracelet."

I laughed. "Hey, I had to make sure that supply of doughnuts keeps coming."

He grinned and shook his head. "You're something else, you know that?"

"So I've been told." I lifted one shoulder in an easy shrug. I was happy and content and falling in love. Life was a rough, bumpy, uncertain road, but when it smoothed out, it was amazingly good. Especially with Sinclair in it. "But there's a lot more to me than what you've seen."

"Oh, I'm sure." He lifted his glass to me. "Here's to discovering it."

I lifted my glass as well, the blissed-out feeling I'd had with him at the ball returning in a smooth easy wave. "Here's to us."

His smile broadened. "That's the best thing I've heard all day."

Want to be up to date on all books & release dates by Kristen Painter? Sign-up for my newsletter on my website, www.kristenpainter.com. No spam, just news (sales, freebies, releases, you know, all that jazz.)

If you loved the book and want to help the series grow, tell a friend about the book and take time to leave a review!

Other Books by Kristen Painter

The Dragon Finds Forever
The Vampire's Accidental Wife

Sin City Collectors series
Queen of Hearts
Dead Man's Hand
Double or Nothing

STAND-ALONE PARANORMAL ROMANCE

Dark Kiss of the Reaper
Heart of Fire
Recipe for Magic
Miss Bramble and the Leviathan

URBAN FANTASY

The House of Comarré series:
Forbidden Blood
Blood Rights
Flesh and Blood
Bad Blood
Out For Blood
Last Blood

Crescent City series:
House of the Rising Sun
City of Eternal Night
Garden of Dreams and Desires

Nothing is completed without an amazing team.

Many thanks to:

Cover design: Keri Knutson
Interior formatting: Author E.M.S.
Editor: Joyce Lamb
Copyedits/proofs: Marlene Engel

About the Author

USA Today Best Selling Author Kristen Painter is a little obsessed with cats, books, chocolate, and shoes. It's a healthy mix. She loves to entertain her readers with interesting twists and unforgettable characters. She currently writes the best-selling paranormal romance series, Nocturne Falls, and award-winning urban fantasy. The former college English teacher can often be found all over social media where she loves to interact with readers

www.kristenpainter.com

Printed in Great Britain
by Amazon

44094623R10169